Libraries
ReadLearn**Connect**

THIS BOOK IS PART OF
ISLINGTON READS BOOKSWAP
SCHEME

Please take this book and either return it to a Bookswap site or replace with one of your own books that you would like to share.

If you enjoy this book, why not join your local Islington Library and borrow more like it for free?

Find out about our FREE e-book, e-audio, newspaper and magazine apps, activities for pre-school children and other services we have to offer at www.islington.gov.uk/libraries

ISLINGTON
For a more equal future

HER
SISTER'S
VOICE

by Lesley Cheetham

LambChop Publishing London WC1

Published by LambChop Publishing, London 2012

Cover Image © Ella Ruth Cowperthwaite
Design by Rosanna Mclaughlin

A catalogue record for this book is available from the British Library

ISBN 978-0-9572858-0-4

For my sister

PROLOGUE

The Voice

The Voice awoke. It had found a new mind to inhabit. It whispered seductively in the girl's ear. She stirred, drowsy in sleep. She listened, froze, then sat bolt upright. The Voice picked up pace, whispering some more. The girl was afraid. The Voice smiled. It had her captive, it was so easy. Now it was time to play.

1

LEILA

The worst thing was we were almost home. Just one more turn at the end of this road and our house would be in sight, an ordinary house with a blue front door, the yellow light behind it warm and inviting. Jenna was dragging behind me; she's always slow. The hole inside me was large tonight, rumbling like an active volcano, urging me along. I stopped suddenly when the familiar buzzing started in my ear and the order came.

Touch the road

I closed my eyes and tried to force it out of my head. The street was dark and lights from the houses stretched like arms out into the road welcoming me in. The Voice pulled me in the other direction towards the dark, dangerous road.

Touch the road then lie down

I offered up a silent resistance, my sister oblivious and trailing behind.

Now!

The loud command propelled me into the road. The tarmac was cold on my bare legs. For a brief, beautiful moment I knew calm. I saw the car's headlights as it turned the corner but I was staying down. It was foolish to resist. A screech, a slam, a furious yell and an angry man shouting at Jenna. She dragged me up out of the road, mortified.

Touch the car bonnet twice

I pulled away from Jenna's grasp and ran to the car and touched it.

'For God's sake' shouted the man, spitting words into the cold air.

'I'm so sorry' said Jenna, white and pinched, grabbing my arm again. This time I didn't resist. I had obeyed and the hole had shrunk back to a manageable proportion. My sister was upset and shaken, but said nothing. She dragged me down the road and pushed me through the blue door, relieved. I ran upstairs, energised and whole again.

2

JENNA

I shut the front door behind me, shaking all over. What the hell had happened there? I cringed with embarrassment when I thought of the driver's face. He must have thought she was drunk or on drugs. Surely that would be easier than being crazy? Should I tell Mum and Dad? Leila would kill me. I hated her for making me feel like this. I didn't know what to do. Nobody had got hurt after all, but what if the road had been busy? Would she have given in to her compulsion? What if the car had been going too fast to stop in time? I had to stop this. I was driving myself insane. If I kept on worrying about Leila the way I had been lately, I would end up like her.

I heard Leila moving about upstairs in our bedroom. We'd always shared a room. It used to be fun, but lately… I went into the kitchen to get a glass of milk. I didn't want to think about it anymore. I would stay downstairs and wait for Mum to bring Lily home. My little sister always cheered me up. We could watch kids TV together. I pretended to only like that stuff for her sake, but secretly I loved it. In fact, why wait for Lily? I could watch whatever I liked.

I switched the TV on and tried to relax on the sofa. My body was still shaking. I sipped at my milk, and tried to calm down. I sent Mary a text then switched my phone onto silent. I didn't feel like chatting. I couldn't tell her anyway, that's what made it so difficult, keeping everything to myself. The sound on the television was turned down low and the picture flickered in front of me. I wasn't watching at all. I was thinking about Leila. Did I ever do anything else these days?

I remember when it all started. Leila was about thirteen at the time. A loud whispering had woken me up one night.

'Jenna! Jenna, quick, wake up!'

'What's the matter?' My heart raced, it must be an emergency.

'I'm scared that I'm going to die. We're all going to die.'

I rubbed my eyes with my fists. What was she on about?

'I don't want to die. Ever. Imagine not being here.'

'I don't believe you. Is that why you've woken me? I thought the house was on fire or something. Worry about being dead when you're old. Now go back to sleep and DON'T wake me up again.'

With that, I had turned over and pointedly pulled the blanket up over my head.

The following morning I was dozing, wondering whether that conversation had been a dream when Leila padded out of bed and touched the wall. She got back into bed. A few minutes later she got back out of bed again and rapped the wall twice with her knuckles, then went into the bathroom. After her shower she came back in and touched the walls again.

'What are you doing?' I asked.

'Nothing' she said 'Mind your own business.'

'Weirdo' I said and went back to sleep.

From that day on she had touched things constantly and developed a twitch in her eyes. My parents didn't take it too seriously and we kind of got used to it; it was just something she did. It became a bit of a family joke, but I noticed Leila had lost some of her spark over the last few months and we weren't as close as we had been. She looked different too; she'd bleached her hair white and wore very dark eye makeup. She looked good, but there was a harder edge to her and sometimes I found her a bit scary, plus she could be a right moody cow. She reeked of smoke too, which upset me as she'd always been dead against smoking.

A noise at the door made me jump back to the present. It was Leila. She looked flushed. 'What have you been doing?' I asked.

'My routine.'

Typical, I thought. That was another of her obsessions. It was a sad DVD that belonged to Mum – a Z list celebrity who had lost weight suddenly and brought out a DVD – before putting the weight back on. I'd seen it before with that girl off Eastenders. What was the point?

'How can you even think about exercise?' I said, incredulously.

'What do you mean?'

'What do I mean? Have you forgotten what just happened out there in the street? You could have been run over.' My heart had started racing again as I pictured Leila lying in the road. Suddenly the ridiculousness of the situation made me burst out laughing. It was only when I felt the wetness of tears running down my face that I realised I was sobbing. Leila crouched down next to me and put her arms around me.

'Stop it, Jenna, stop it. I don't know what to do.'

'Neither do I!' I shouted. 'Now you know how I feel. I

need to talk to Mum' I sobbed.

She grabbed me by the shoulders. 'No, Jenna' she gasped. 'Please, you mustn't.'

'Then tell me why you did that! What if I had lain down in the street like that? What would you think?'

She sat back on her heels and looked at me, biting her lip. I was calming down now. At least I had her attention. She so rarely talked to me these days.

'Jenna I...'

I waited for her to give me her secrets. I knew the words were on the tip of her tongue. I could tell by the way her forehead crinkled up in concentration. I could almost see the thoughts whizzing around inside her head. I willed her to speak.

Suddenly, she jumped to her feet and the mood was shattered.

'You'll just have to trust me' she said. 'It's something I have to do. I can't tell you, so don't keep asking me. But if you tell Mum I will never, ever forgive you.'

She was staring down at me and the look on her face cut right through me. A chill crept through my bones.

'Ok' I stammered. 'I won't.' What else could I do? My pulse was still fluttering and I willed myself to calm down. Was I really frightened of my own sister?

'Promise me' she insisted, her flashing eyes boring into mine. I nodded my head frantically. I had a feeling I was going to regret this promise.

3

LEILA

On the bus home from school snatches of conversation filtered through into my mind. A giggle. Girls laughing. The bus was rammed with school kids letting off steam after a day pent up at school. I didn't notice the noise as I was so wrapped up in my thoughts. People really got on my nerves lately. My teacher had asked me why I was so quiet today. I didn't tell her that my head was full of cotton wool and tears sprang out of my eyes for no reason. And the man's voice from last night was still ringing in my ears, 'She needs locking up.' I couldn't risk speaking to anyone in case I let slip about The Voice. I was too scared. Besides, she would have thought I was nuts.

The bus jolted as the driver came to an abrupt halt at a red light and I snapped out of my thoughts. The laughter was right behind me. Sighing, I immediately assumed it was directed at me. I twitched my head again. It was stupid to hope other people wouldn't notice. The laughter got louder. Suddenly I heard my name being called.

'Leila.'

Should I respond? It would only make it worse if I ignored them. I turned around. Four girls from my year were sitting a few rows back. Three of them started nodding their heads to the side, in unison. They'd obviously been practising.

'Have you got nits?' the fourth girl asked, 'Is that why you keep shaking your head?'

They burst out laughing. I'd had enough. The bus was a couple of stops away from where I would normally get off but I'd rather walk than sit through any more humiliation. I grabbed my bag and headed for the stairs. As I passed the girls they started bobbing their heads again.

'Piss off' I shouted and ran down the stairs.

When I got home Mum was in the kitchen and my little sister Lily was drawing in her book at the kitchen table. When she saw me she jumped up and threw herself at me. 'Will you help me with my drawing?' she asked.

I was too fired up to sit still.

'Sorry' I said, pushing her gently away. 'I've got stuff to do.' Her face dropped.

'Leila' said Mum, 'surely you can spend five minutes with your sister.'

'I haven't got time, Mum' I said, 'I've got homework to do, alright.' Mum was so annoying at times. She always got my back up. I went off upstairs, hating myself for upsetting Lily – again. Now I needed a cigarette to calm me down. I'd have to sneak out to the park later, before it got dark.

Alone in my bedroom I took 'Heidi' down from the bookshelf. My old favourite was battered and worn as I had read it so many times. I needed to escape from the thoughts crashing around in my head. I realised it was ages since I had read a book. After five minutes I put it down, exasperated. Why couldn't I concentrate? Mum used to tell me off for always having my nose stuck in a book. What was wrong with me?

Out of the corner of my eye something flickered. I turned to look at the window. Was it windy outside? The street light cast a long dark shadow on the wall. It was slinky like a long match-stick figure. At the same time The Voice started up in my head. It was hissing; I couldn't make out the words. I tried to shut it out. The shadow moved, making me jump. What was it?

At that moment the bedroom door opened and Jenna came in. The shadow vanished and my head cleared.

'Guess what?' she announced breathlessly. 'Some new people are moving in next door.'

'About time' I said, grateful for the distraction. 'It's been ages since Mr Jones died.'

'I don't like living next to an empty house. What if Mr Jones's ghost is in there? I'm sure I can hear noises at night.'

'Don't be silly' I said. 'Ghosts don't exist.' *Except in my head.* 'Did Mum say who is moving in?'

'No, but I hope there is someone my age. None of my friends live round here. Hey, what about a hunky boy for you?' teased Jenna. 'Wouldn't you like to have a boyfriend?'

'Get lost' I said. 'Boys are a waste of space. Besides, I've got too much coursework to do. I know I'm going to fail my maths.' I just couldn't get maths. I worried about it a lot. I hated it when I couldn't get things right. A boyfriend would be a distraction, the last thing I needed right now. The Voice was bad enough. Anxiety ripped through me and I could feel my face dancing, grimacing.

'Leila' said Jenna 'don't do that. It looks silly.'

'Get lost' I snapped. 'It's none of your business.' I regretted it immediately but the damage was done. Jenna's face fell and she got off the bed and went downstairs without saying a word. Great. Now I had upset both my sisters. I threw the book on the floor and plugged my earphones in. Hopefully music would drown out my thoughts and help stop me twitching.

The earphones were making a buzzing noise. I couldn't hear any music. I pulled the buds out of my ears to see what was wrong when a gust of wind burst into the room. I looked up and gasped. The shadow that had caught my eye earlier was back. It was definitely a long thin shape, like a person. I couldn't see what was causing it.

Stop resisting

The Voice. I should have realised. Every time I tried to push it away it got worse, just like the things it was making me do got worse and ever more complicated.

'I'm tired, leave me alone.' I whispered.

Stop resisting and accept the inevitable. You must move and count and do exactly as I tell you. You know what will happen otherwise.

A throbbing started up in my head. I nodded. I knew what I had to do. I lay back on the bed and started counting backwards from one thousand, my eyes fixed on the ceiling. Slowly, the throbbing ebbed away and the shadow vanished from the room. I was safe again, but for how long?

4

JENNA

Wow! I threw myself down on my bed, grinning madly. Did that really happen? I hadn't been home from school long and was lying on my bed chatting to Mary on my phone when Mum had called me downstairs.

'I'll call you back' I said to Mary. She carried on chatting but I'd already cut her off. I ran downstairs then slowed my pace as I realised Mum was talking to a woman on the doorstep. I cursed her under my breath for not giving me any warning. I never know what to say to new people. I ran my fingers through my curls and smoothed my skirt down as I reached the front door.

'This is Helen' said Mum.

She was tall, with chestnut coloured hair and a smiley face. I liked her instantly. I needn't have worried about what to say as Helen talked without stopping. Even Mum struggled to get a word in. Mum is bossy and organises the local neighbourhood committee – maybe she had finally met her match. Within minutes I knew that Helen was married to John, worked as a freelance journalist and had a baby daughter, Olivia and a nineteen year old stepdaughter who no longer lived at home. She turned to me and gave me a big smile.

'I also have a son' she said. 'He's about your age' she said. 'Wait there a sec….' before I had time to realise what was happening she had disappeared next door and was back seconds later with a boy in tow. He looked as embarrassed as I felt. 'Charlie' she said 'Meet…'

'Jenna' I said, realising Mum hadn't told her my name. 'Hi' I said, pushing back the annoying strand of stupidly curly hair that had fallen down over my eye.

'Hi' he replied and looked at me and we both smiled nervously. I wanted the ground to swallow me up. I didn't know what else to say. He was actually pretty good looking and here I was acting like a complete numbskull. Mum and I waved as they went back into their house, then she shut the door behind us.

'What a friendly woman,' she said, 'I've invited her round for coffee tomorrow. It will be nice to get to know our new neighbours.' I was one hundred per cent in agreement. In fact, I rushed upstairs to my bedroom, where I got straight back on the phone to Mary.

I was struggling to get my breath after taking the stairs two at a time when Mary answered on the first ring.

'Why are you breathing heavily?' she asked. 'Please don't tell me you've joined your crazy sister in her fitness routine?'

'As if!' I said 'You'll never guess what?'

'I'm waiting' she said. I could picture her on the other end of the phone winding her long fair hair around her finger, as she always does when she's concentrating.

'I've just met our next door neighbours.'

'And?' she said. 'Spill the details.'

I stretched out on the bed, looking up at the ceiling.

'Well' I said. 'There's Helen and John, they're like, old – mum and dad's age, and they have a son Charlie – and he's cute!' I babbled excitedly. 'He's about fifteen and he's quite tall, with light brown hair and brown eyes, and he's muscly, as if he works out or something and he's got a lovely wide smile. He's even got freckles.'

'Well that's it then' said Mary. 'If he's got freckles…'

'Shut up'

'Did you speak to him?'

'Mum introduced me and he said 'Hi.''

'Is that it? Didn't you even have a conversation?' Mary's Irish accent got stronger when she raised her voice.

'I can't explain it – you know when you first meet some-one and you just know that you like them? Well he's nice, not arrogant like most boys.'

'Do you even know any boys?'

She was right; I hardly mixed with boys since we had left primary school.

'Look, I like him alright.'

'Love is in the air …' sang Mary

'Oh get lost. As a friend I mean. Listen to me, I don't even know him.'

'So will I be seeing you this weekend, or will you be hanging around with the boy next door now?'

Mary and I always got together on Saturdays even though we lived on opposite sides of town.

'I'll be seeing you, why wouldn't I? Now let me get on with my homework.'

Next day on my way to school I had a spring in my step. Charlie Birch. That was his name. I hoped we were going to be friends. I was still thinking about the new neighbours later that day when I bumped into Leila in the corridor. She was being given a real telling off by one of her teachers for pulling faces during lesson. Leila was staring at her blankly as if she had no idea what the woman was talking about. I hadn't given Leila much thought today – that made a nice change.

The teacher was referring to the faces Leila had started pulling. I remember the first time. She was sitting on her bed sorting out her schoolbag. Suddenly she went very still, looked up at the ceiling and then pulled a face. It happened so fast I wouldn't have thought anything of it, but then she did it again – and again.

'Leila' I said. 'What are you doing?' She looked at me and pulled the face twice at lightning speed.

'What?'

I felt sick. I had a sinking feeling that some new craziness was starting here.

'What?' she repeated and pulled the face again.

'Don't you know what you are doing?' I asked.

She looked at me questioningly. 'What are you talking about? I'm unpacking my bag.'

I stared at her. She did it again.

'Leila' I said 'You're pulling funny faces.'

'Just ignore it.'

'But Leila' I protested. 'It looks ridiculous.'

'Shut up' she said, her eyes flashing angrily at me between twitches. 'You know there are some things I have to do.'

'But...'

'I can't talk about it; you know that, so stop hassling me.'

'Leila...'

'Jenna, I've warned you before. It's none of your business ok.'

I hated her when she spoke to me sharply like that. I got up and went downstairs to find Lily. She was lying on the living room drawing a picture.

'What are you drawing Lily?' I asked.

'A monkey. We're going to the zoo with school tomorrow. I want to draw all the animals that I'm going to see. Do you want to draw one?'

'A giraffe' I said. 'Pass me some pencils.'

'I asked Leila to draw with me but she said no. Then she pulled a face at me. Why is she always cross?'

'She probably has a lot of homework to do. I'm sure she wanted to draw really. And she wasn't pulling faces at you, it's a twitch – she can't help it. Just ignore it.'

We all ignored the face and after a while I barely noticed it. I did ask Mum once if she thought Leila was all right, but she said it was nothing to worry about; Leila had a touch of OCD but she thought she would soon grow out of it. I wasn't so sure.

I really liked Charlie. I pretended that I didn't but I found myself wondering about him and what he was up to. I watched him go off to school every morning, walking in the opposite direction from the one that I took, strolling casually with his bag slung on his back. Charlie went to the mixed school – trust Mum to make us go to the stupid girls' school. I hated school and spent the whole week longing for the weekend. It was worse since Charlie moved in. I'd been told off in class for not paying attention and that was a first.

'Jenna that's twice this week you've been told off!' Mary was teasing me at the end of school one day. 'Are you dreaming about the boy next door by any chance?'

'No.' I lied. 'Anyway, there's no point. He's bound to have

loads of girls after him. But I am looking forward to going home today. We're going next door to meet baby Olivia. If nothing else it will make a change from Mum and Leila arguing. Mum doesn't like the fact that Leila is round at Samia's house all the time or upstairs in her bedroom and she never has much time for Lily. Lily gets upset about it. Mum goes on at Leila, then Leila yells at Mum. I'm getting sick of it.'

I said goodbye to Mary and set off home. Secretly I thought that a really cute boy moving in next door was the best thing that could have happened. I could dream, couldn't I?

5

LEILA

I pressed the doorbell and stood back expectantly. It was a relief to have got there at last. Already evening was closing in, the sky dark and oppressive, the streetlights were on and it was only five pm. My mood dropped down a gear. Although Samia's house was only a twenty-minute walk from my own, the journey was taking me longer and longer each time I came over. There were so many things to touch and number plates to memorise plus I had to keep stopping and retracing my steps, to make sure I had remembered them correctly.

Samia and Cherry are my best friends and they are both in the same tutor group as me at school. Samia and I see more of one another out of school, as Cherry is always busy running around after her little brother since her dad left home last year.

The curtains were drawn but I could see that the lights were on already. I loved spending time at Samia's house. She had a lot more freedom than I did. Her dad was always at work and her mum mostly left us to our own devices when I was there. The sound of feet running down the stairs awoke me from my daydream and Samia opened the door with her hair wrapped in a towel.

'Come up quick' she said, 'I need to wash this conditioner off my hair.'

Samia disappeared into the bathroom and I headed straight up to her bedroom. It was a loft conversion and she had only recently moved in there. It was accessible through a tiny wooden staircase and was a great place to hang out. It felt really secluded, away from the prying eyes of parents and Samia's little sister and brother.

Samia had a full-length mirror in her room and I grimaced as I caught sight of myself in it. I took off my jacket and threw it on the bed. Music was pumping out of the speakers and it lifted my spirits a little; it was our current favourite, a compilation of 1960's girl groups. Samia and I shared an obsession with sixties fashion and were currently experimenting with black eyeliner, false lashes and beehives. The beehive was the trickiest. Samia's thick black hair was no trouble to sweep up into position, but my straight blonde hair was less accommodating.

I didn't have a full length mirror at home so I always took advantage of Samia's to see how I looked. I stood up tall and sucked in my stomach. I was average looking with shoulder length blonde hair, and up until recently had always been slim, despite having the appetite of a horse. I had a really sweet tooth, unlike Samia who didn't seem that interested in food and was naturally very thin. Cherry also had a gorgeous figure and both my friends were way taller than me. I had felt my body growing lately but unfortunately not in an upwards direction. All through primary school I'd been teased about being so small and people would always cuff me on the head in a patronising manner, which drove me mad. After a series of eruptions on my part, nobody did that any more. I stood and looked face on at the mirror. Looking at myself lately made me feel sick. I was starting to get way too curvy. Samia said she was jealous – as if I could believe that! I would give anything to look like Samia. Samia's father was Asian and her mother was Scottish and she had long black shiny hair and beautiful bone structure, inherited from her dad. Then there was my own sister – Jenna was slim and had lovely dark curly hair, which she didn't like but I adored it. Jenna had always been a fussy eater and I couldn't imagine her developing suddenly in the way that I had.

'Hey stop admiring yourself girl' Samia said as she came into the room, rubbing her hair dry with the towel. 'Wait till you see my new trousers, they're awesome. I used the H & M voucher dad gave me for my birthday last week; I knew it wouldn't last long.' Samia rummaged in her wardrobe and pulled out a carrier bag. She took out a pair of skinny grey cord trousers and held them up against her. 'Do you want to see them on?' Without waiting for an answer she slipped off her skirt and pulled the trousers on, sliding them easily over her slim hips. Lately I had had to struggle to get my favourite jeans over my thighs and I felt a pang of envy.

'Well?' asked Samia, 'Let me walk down the runway for you, pretend I'm on Britain's Next Top Model.'

As she sashayed across the room, pouting and sticking her tiny bum out at me as she posed at the end of her imaginary runway, I couldn't help laughing. I mentally batted away the negative thoughts and smiled.

'You look gorgeous, but when are you going to wear them?'

'Now's as good a time as any! I thought we could go into town, grab a burger and go to the park? What do you think?'

'Great' I said, 'but I'll pass on the burger. I had a huge meal before I came out.' I was a bit surprised to find the lie rolling out of my mouth so easily. I didn't think I'd ever lied to Samia before. Seeing myself like that in the mirror had given me a bit of a shock, so skipping a meal wouldn't do any harm. 'A huge diet coke with ice would be good though,' I added quickly, to stop myself sounding like a total killjoy. 'And on the way there I'll tell you what happened at school today, when you were at the dentist. There was a big fight between Kelsey and Julia.'

We linked arms and set off down the street. It was fully dark now.

'So come on' Samia said impatiently.

'Well, this is Cherry's version' I said, 'as it started out in technology and I wasn't in that lesson. You know the new girl, Kelsey?'

'You mean Kelsey the moody Goth? Do I know her? Don't you remember I had to look after her during her first week at school? That was a barrel of laughs. She barely spoke to me.'

I laughed. 'So during technology Kelsey told Mr Collins that Marcia was making fun of her. Mr Collins told them both to stop being childish and basically ignored it. Then when the bell went, Cherry was in the playground and she saw Marcia go up to Kelsey and start having a go at her. Next minute they were both rolling about in the grass.'

'I wouldn't fancy Marcia's chances in a fight – Kelsey is huge.'

'Everyone came rushing over – you know what it's like – the year sevens were screaming at them. It wasn't much of a fight really; mostly scratching and pulling each other's hair. Then Mr Collins and Miss Saleem marched in and spoilt the fun. They both got dragged off to the Head of Year's office. Marcia had a big scratch on her cheek and was swearing at Kelsey. She'll probably get excluded – again.'

'I knew it! Marcia is pretty nasty and she probably was making fun of Kelsey, but I've always thought that Kelsey is full of rage. She takes everything in, you know. She's dark and mysterious. Hey, I bet she's a vampire. I'm going to make sure I don't sit next to her in class in case she takes a chunk out of my neck.'

'Idiot!' I pushed Samia playfully and she pushed me back.

'Trust me to miss out on all the excitement. I think I need an extra-large burger to make up for it.' She pulled away from me and ran off ahead. 'Last one to the end of the road has to pay!'

'You're on' I shouted and set off in hot pursuit after her.

The Voice

The game had begun. The girl had understood the message and doubts were setting in. Let the self-destruction commence...

6

JENNA

I was singing along to my iPod, stretched out on my bed. I had gone next door with Mum to meet Helen's baby girl, Olivia. Olivia was so sweet. Helen let me hold her and she fell asleep in my arms, after giving me a big, gummy smile and dribbling all over my hand. That was the state I was in on the sofa, when Charlie came in. I could have died.

'Hi' he said. His face was flushed and he was wearing sports gear. I knew he had been to his gymnastics club as Helen had told me earlier. 'I see you've met Olivia.'

I looked down at Olivia. I couldn't help smiling at her funny expression. 'She's great' I said. 'Apart from dribbling all over me.' It was easier to talk to him looking down at Olivia. Looking up at his face made me feel all flustered and tongue-tied.

'How was gym?' I asked, smoothing Olivia's hair behind her ear. She gurgled in her sleep.

'Good. We're training for a competition next month. I've got a routine to learn so I had to really concentrate. I think I've almost got it now.'

'Have you been going for long?' I asked, looking up at

him for the first time. He had a smattering of freckles over the top of his nose and his eyes were a warm shade of brown.

'Since I was five' he said. 'Mum used to take me every week and sit and chat to the other mums. To be honest, I can't remember ever not doing gymnastics. Good job I like it. Do you do any sport?'

I dreaded him asking me that question. PE was probably my least favourite subject and I couldn't catch a ball to save my life. I shook my head. 'I like watching it on TV' I said, 'Does that count?'

He laughed. 'Sure. I like watching running and athletics but I don't understand all the fuss about football. Boys are supposed to be born liking it but I've never really got it. Dad's disappointed, I know.'

I liked him more and more. Football was a mystery to me too.

'When Mum was pregnant with Olivia Dad was convinced she was having a boy. I know he was fantasising about taking him to football matches with him.'

'Girls like football too. Leila does.'

'Dad's a bit old fashioned. Is Leila your sister?'

'Yes, the older one. Lily is my younger sister, she's eight.'

'I've got an older step sister, Molly' said Charlie. 'She doesn't live with us.' A shadow passed across his face. 'What's your school like?'

We chatted for a bit about school and I was telling him about my friends and what there was to do in town – not much – and I was amazed at how easy he was to talk to. I didn't know many boys, apart from my cousins and they were way too nerdy to count. There were a few boys I liked – Jacob from Twilight, Aston from JLS – but none I'd ever met. I had posters of Jacob all over my side of the bedroom. Mary was the same – you couldn't even see her bedroom walls for pictures of boy bands. Leila thought I was sad. The posters on her side of the room were all black and white movie stars, mainly female. She spent hours practicing her makeup and hair, trying to perfect old fashioned looks which had gone full circle and were back in fashion again.

'Your sister is quite scary looking' Charlie was saying. 'She was smoking in the bus shelter the other day and I was wondering whether to say hello. She was giving me evil looks so I decided against it.'

I sighed. I hated Leila smoking. 'She's not scary' I said, 'but she can be pretty intense …' *and sometimes she is downright weird*. I kept that thought to myself – I didn't want to frighten him off. I wondered how Charlie saw me. I wasn't over the moon with my looks, but I wonder if any girl is? Obviously there was the problem with my ridiculously curly hair which everybody else liked but they didn't have to live with it. If I got caught in the rain I looked like a mad scarecrow. I had way too many freckles and my skin was beyond fair. At primary school Mum was forever getting calls from school saying I wasn't well because I was so pale! I was tall and skinny and no matter what I ate I never put any weight on. Leila said I was lucky but she was the lucky one, she had a gorgeous figure with curves in all the right places, straight hair and long eyelashes and I tried to convince myself that as I got older my body would develop in the same way as hers.

Charlie was slightly older than me and really fit. He couldn't be interested in me, could he? He was probably just being polite. I tried to concentrate on what he was saying and not reveal to him the jabbering idiot that was lurking beneath the surface.

Mum and Helen came into the room, still chatting. Olivia wriggled and let out an almighty wail. 'Typical' said Helen, 'Olivia wakes up as soon as I come into the room.' She reached over and took her out of my arms.

'She's adorable' I said. 'Do you have a babysitter?'
Helen laughed. 'Only Charlie and he's way too dreamy. I worry he'll go out and forget all about her.'

Charlie rolled his eyes. 'Mum' he said, 'you're so embarrassing. I'm fifteen now. But Jenna can come over and keep me company if it makes you feel better.'

I nodded, trying not to grin from ear to ear.

'Come on Jenna' said Mum. 'I wouldn't take it personally, Charlie. I still worry about leaving Lily with my husband. She's probably running riot next door.'

Helen followed Mum out of the room and I got up to go after them.

'Do you fancy coming over this weekend' asked Charlie, 'to watch a DVD?'

I swallowed hard. 'Great' I said, trying to look like boys asked me to watch DVD's every day of my life. 'See you then.'

I followed Mum out, resisting the urge to skip. My stomach had been doing cartwheels ever since. I couldn't believe it. There were a million questions running through my head. Would he have invited me if he was just being polite? Maybe his mum had told him to be nice to me? Since then I had been lying on my bed, listening to music and replaying the evening in my head. I was trying unsuccessfully to think about something else when Leila came in. She went through her usual ritual of touching the wall, the cupboard and the light switch, before sitting down on the end of my bed.

'Hey' I said, trying to appear normal. 'Where have you

been?'

'I had a burger in town with Sami' she said. 'Then we went to the park and sat on the swings for a bit, nothing special.

'I went next door with Mum. Baby Olivia is adorable and I am going to be her baby sitter. With Charlie' I added.

'Charlie? The cute one?' Leila squealed. 'Jenna don't tell me you've got a boyfriend?'

'Don't be stupid' I said. My face felt really hot. I didn't want her to know how I felt. Luckily she started telling me about a fight that had happened at school between two girls in her year. I had heard something had happened and for a moment I forgot all about Charlie too.

'Is Kelsey the Goth girl?' I asked. Leila nodded. 'What's she like? She doesn't seem very friendly.'

'She's not' said Leila. 'I don't like her much, but I'm not sure why. Samia reckons she's a vampire! I heard she wanted to go to Larksmead. I don't know why she came to Stenfield Academy. She obviously doesn't like it, she always looks miserable.'

'I don't think you get to choose which school you go to these days. Maybe she lives in the wrong catchment area? You know some rich parents move just so they can get their kids into a certain school? That's an idea actually. Let's persuade Mum and Dad to move to a remote part of the country so we can't go to school. That would be great!' As I was voicing my thoughts I realised that I would only be happy with this if Charlie was still able to live next door. The thought surprised me – I had only just met him. 'As long as we could still see our friends' I added.

Leila gave me a strange look and climbed off the bed. 'And how exactly would that be good?' she pouted. 'I'd hate to be far away from school. I get to see my friends every day there and we have a laugh. It would be awful to be stuck in the country.

It's bad enough here at weekends, there's so little to do and everything closes early, not like in London. I hate it.' She was right. Stenfield was pretty boring. Officially it's in Greater London, but there's nothing remotely great about it. Parts of it are very green and pretty as it borders on the countryside. Old people love it here; young people can't wait to escape.

I sat and watched her as she moved around the bedroom, getting herself ready for bed, eyes and mouth twitching as she went into the bathroom. She pulled faces constantly now. I wondered if Charlie had noticed her twitches. I was used to it but I had seen the way people looked at her at school, nudging each other, copying her and laughing. I hated them for it. Mary always dragged me away – not that I would ever say anything, I wouldn't dare. But it upset me to see my sister being laughed at. Leila came out of the bathroom with her pyjamas on and lay down on the floor. What was she doing now? I expected the unexpected with her these days. She put her hands behind her head and raised her top half off the floor. Sit-ups. I counted as she did two hundred without stopping. Another routine I would have to get used to. This would be a nightly ritual now. There was no going back with Leila once she had started something.

7

LEILA

School had been crap today and I was in a foul mood. I'd been trying really hard for the last two months to stop myself pulling faces, as the headaches it gave me were making it difficult for me to concentrate in class. I rubbed my forehead.

'Are you ok?' Samia had asked me at lunchtime.

I shook my head and groaned.

'Bad head.' I lowered my voice. 'And I need a cigarette.'

'Honestly Leila. It's so bad for you. You'll get caught. I bet your mum doesn't know, does she?'

I shook my head. I wanted to tell her how it eased the knots of anxiety in my stomach, but stopped myself.

'What lesson have we got next?'

'Maths.'

'That's all I need. Maybe I should bunk off. Why does maths have to be compulsory? I'm going to fail the exam.'

'It would help if we had a better teacher. Bakewell Tart is crap.'

Samia was right. Mrs Bakewell wasn't the best teacher, but maths worried me – all my other results were going to be good. My mind went blank when faced with numbers.

'Don't forget you've got detention tonight.' Samia reminded me.

I groaned. The day went from bad to worse. I had forgotten. I was aware of my face jumping up and down, but had no energy to stop it.

'It's so unfair. I sit next to Julia because she is good at maths and she offered to help me, then I get detention for talking. What's that about? Teachers hate me.'

'No they don't.'

'Yes they do.' Samia didn't know that Mrs Berger had told me to stop twitching 'my fat little face' this morning. I was gutted. Was my face fat?

'My head is killing me Sami' I moaned.

She stood up. 'Come on; let's go down to reception before the bell goes. Get you some paracetemol.'

We linked arms and pushed our way down the corridor.

'Mind where you're going' shouted a girl as I brushed against her. I cringed. I was so fat and clumsy.

I was tempted to skip detention but my headache had improved a little by the end of the day, so I decided to get it over with, reluctantly making my way up to the maths room. The maths department was in the old Victorian school block, which was only accessible by a narrow staircase. I ran up the stairs two steps at a time – more exercise might help me stay in shape. Mrs Berger's comment was still preying on my mind. The teacher wasn't there when I arrived, so I quickly did an about turn and ran back down the stairs so that I could repeat the exercise. Just as I turned to run up the stairs for the second time I noticed Kelsey Atwood coming in behind me. I forced myself to smile, trying not to pant. Just what I needed.

Kelsey shifted about awkwardly. She loomed over me; I'd forgotten how tall she was. She definitely could do with running up and down the stairs.

'Have you got detention?' she asked. I wondered how she got away with making her uniform look so Goth like. Her makeup was very dark; I always wore eyeliner and mascara, but hers was way more dramatic. Her lank hair pulled her face down. I nodded. A clicking of heels announced the arrival of Ms Saleem and I hurried into the classroom. I threw my bag down on the chair next to me to make sure Kelsey didn't sit there.

She lumbered in and sat down at the desk diagonally in front of me and Miss Saleem told us to get on with homework that had been set in the lesson earlier. I spent most of the next half hour watching numbers dance about in front of me. Every time I looked up, Kelsey was staring blankly at me. I shuddered and turned away from her.

As soon as the clock read four o'clock I was out of there. As I pushed through the door, I heard Kelsey calling me. Reluctantly I paused.

'What is it?' I snapped, 'I'm in a hurry.'

She cleared her throat.

'Kelsey?' I said.

She stared at me. 'Oh it's nothing,' she said, turned abruptly and shuffled off in the opposite direction.

I stared at her retreating back. She was so weird. Anger and frustration chewed knots in my stomach. I turned and started to run. I felt like a pressure cooker, about to explode.

I smoked a cigarette in the bus shelter, before letting myself into the house. I rushed upstairs, not stopping to speak to anyone and studied my face in the bedroom mirror. Was it fat? I had an average kind of face and had long ago accepted that I'd never be beautiful, but I supposed that as my body was growing and changing, and it had certainly been doing that lately, that maybe my face had got fat and I had been so busy that I had failed to notice.

'Leila' Mum called up the stairs. 'Dinner in half an hour, ok?'

I opened the door and shouted over the bannister.

'Thanks Mum.' I would talk to her about it later. The thought cheered me up and I did some homework until I heard Mum calling me down for dinner.

'Coming' I shouted and went downstairs two at a time. I was pleased as Mum was alone; Dad was at work and Jenna had taken Lily next door. That would make it easier to talk to her. I was hungry and exhausted. Trying so hard to stop twitching was really taking it out of me. Mum would understand.

'Mum.'

'Yes dear?' she had already started eating her food and seemed to be in a hurry. She chewed rapidly. 'I'm going to Pilates with Helen from next door. It's a new class, but I'm running late as usual. Are you ok?'

I nodded. 'Mum, I wanted to ask you something…'

'Oh no' she said, slapping her hand to her forehead. 'I forgot to phone the optician. What time does he close?'

I couldn't believe it. How was I supposed to know? There was nothing wrong with my eye sight. I wished there was, then I wouldn't be able to see myself so clearly. I tried again.

'The thing is Mum…'

'I think they stay open until six. I'm sorry Leila, I'm going to have to ring the opticians before they close. You eat your food up, there's a good girl.' She pushed her chair back and went out into the hall.

I was fuming. It didn't take much for Mum to annoy me lately but tonight I had needed her. She never had time for me. I looked down at my plate. The food that had looked so appetising when I first came down for dinner had lost its appeal. Mum would expect me to clear my plate because I always did. Jenna and Lily were the fussy eaters. A light went on in my head. It struck me with crystal clarity. The only thing I did right – one hundred per cent right in my mother's eyes – was eat my bloody dinner. Good girl, greedy old Leila, I ate it all up obediently, while my sisters fretted and fussed and shifted the food around their plates because there were so many things they didn't like. No wonder I had a fat face. Well I can play at that game too, I decided. And I'll be better than everyone else at it. I put down my knife and fork. And stopped eating.

8

JENNA

Mary and I were eating our lunch outside the gym at school. I'd traded my last cheese and pickle sandwich for her bag of salt and vinegar crisps. We were sat on the floor huddled up in our coats and scarves in an attempt to beat the wind. Noise from the playground drifted over but it was quieter where we were. I leant back against the wall and shook the crumbs off my coat.

'Leila's driving me mad' I said. 'Last night I wanted to do my homework up in the bedroom where Lily can't disturb me, but she wouldn't let me in because she was exercising. She's mad. I hardly ever see her these days – when she's not locked in the bedroom she goes round to Samia's – I can't remember the last time we were all at home together. As for eating dinner like we used to, that never happens. She rushes around all the time. Is your sister like that?'

'Oh exactly' she said. 'It's the GCSE's. The whole of year eleven are totally stressed, haven't you noticed? Martha is the same; she's always up in her room studying. She never watches

TV with me like she used to. No way am I going to be like that when I do my GCSE's – and I hope you aren't either.'

'I suppose you're right. It must be really stressful. School's bad enough as it is, without exams.'

'Well I wouldn't worry about Leila' said Mary. 'It's a phase. She'll be back to normal once the exams are over, I bet you.'

'Some chance' I said, 'Leila's never been normal.'

I was lying in bed later thinking about what Mary had said. She was usually right, but Martha didn't look washed out like Leila did. Leila was still awake; I could hear her thrashing about.

'Lee' I said 'Is everything ok? You seem so busy lately; we hardly ever see each other.'

'Of course it is' she said. 'I just have loads of schoolwork and you know I like hanging out round Samia's. Her mum is so chilled out, unlike ours.'

'Oh Mum's not that bad' I said, leaping to her defence. 'I think she just worries about you. She can't help it, that's what mum's do. She wants to protect us – I feel the same about Lily.'

'Lily is eight' said Leila. 'I am nearly grown up. I'll be sixteen soon. I'm fed up with being treated like a little kid. Samia's mum lets her go to bed whenever she likes, they don't have all these stupid rules that we do, like bedtimes and mealtimes.'

'You never come home for dinner anymore either, Lee. I can't remember the last time we all ate together at the same time.'

'You sound like Mum! I hate doing everything as a family' Leila snapped. 'Lily's so noisy she drives me mad. Anyway, you can't talk; you always seem to be next door these days.'

I was glad she couldn't see me blushing. It was true; I was getting on really well with Charlie. He was so easy to talk to, which made a welcome change from Leila. I was discovering that boys could be good friends too, just in a different way.

'It's nothing to do with you' she said more gently. 'I know I can talk to you at night if I want to. We've always done that haven't we? Do you remember when we used to spend half the night playing silly games and Mum was always coming in to tell us to go to sleep? And that time you got your hair caught up in a hairbrush and I had to go and get her as you got so scared you would have to cut it off? I was more scared of what Mum would say.' Leila giggled, and then she was quiet for a while. Outside there was suddenly a lot of noise; voices and laughter and car doors slamming. The pub across the road was closing.

'Jen' she said quietly, 'don't you think it was more fun when we were little, that things were so much easier and you didn't have to worry about anything?'

'How do you mean?' I asked.

Leila was silent for a moment. 'I often get this feeling in my stomach, when I feel sort of afraid and I panic and I don't know how to get rid of it. Smoking helps, I know you don't approve, but it makes me feel less anxious. That's why I keep myself busy, then I don't have time to worry.'

'Is that why you touch things? Is it a superstitious thing?'

There was a longer silence. I stared unseeing into the darkness and waited.

'If I tell you will you promise not to laugh at me?' she said, whispering so quietly, I could barely hear her.

'I won't laugh at you.'

She took a deep breath. 'I have to do things.'

'Like what?'

'Touch things, count things, arrange things. You know

45

that.' I nodded, despite the pitch black between us. 'And sometimes, I have bad thoughts, where I have to do something that I know I shouldn't. It's as if somebody is telling me what to do. I know it isn't right, but I can't say no.'

'Can't you just ignore it?' I asked. It seemed simple to me.

She laughed. 'I wish. That's the problem. The thought doesn't go away. It keeps coming back until I give in. If I don't do what it says then something bad will happen. To you, or Lily, or Mum and Dad. Don't you see? I have to keep you safe. That's why you mustn't tell.'

I sighed inwardly. I was more worried now than I had been half an hour ago and I wished I didn't have to promise not to tell. But Leila was my big sister and I was used to doing what she wanted.

'Look,' she said. 'I am trying to beat this thing. I've been trying hard not to pull faces, haven't you noticed? I'll do it less, I swear. That way, you don't need to tell Mum, ok?'

I wasn't happy and it took me ages to get to sleep. Her words were echoing in my ears. I didn't like the sound of a voice telling her what to do. What if it told her to do something really bad? I shuddered. I sat up and had a drink of water, trying in vain to think about something else. What could be causing the emptiness she described? It scared me. I didn't want her to stop telling me stuff, but I wished she would talk to someone older who knew how to help her. Not her worried little sister who didn't have a clue what she should do about it.

9

LEILA

'Are you coming to lunch Leila?' Cherry was packing her stuff away at the end of lesson. 'No, I'm going to the library. I need to finish my coursework. Anyway, the school canteen is rubbish. You know I'm only eating healthy stuff now.'

'Oh go on, it's chips today.'

'No way' I said, grimacing.

'You'll soon get fed up with all those vegetables.'

'What are you dieting for anyway? You don't need to lose weight.' Samia had caught the end of the conversation.

'I'm not dieting, I'm just following a healthy eating plan.'

'So why are you still smoking then?' asked Samia.

'Oh shut up.' I said. 'I can't be perfect.'

'Well you say you're not dieting but you've definitely lost weight. Come on Samia, let's go before the queue gets too long.'

I was thrilled. I knew I had lost weight but that was the first time anyone had noticed. I was aiming to get my first pair of skinny jeans, size eight, as soon as I could lose enough.

Mum was a bit funny about my new diet, so it was easier to get my own meals.

'Girls your age don't need to diet' she said. 'And I wish you wouldn't shut yourself up in the bedroom, so much. You should get out with your friends more.' Jenna made fun of me too for exercising. What I needed, was a kindred spirit. There must be other people out there who felt like I did. You can find anything on the Internet these days. I logged onto Google and thought about what I actually wanted. I was so used to pretending to other people that it felt good to be able to say honestly what was on my mind. After a few moments concentration my fingers danced lightly across the keyboard:

'I need to be thinner'

I thought that pretty much summed up what I was feeling right now. A string of websites lined up before me. I clicked one at random and started reading.

Half an hour later I sat back, my mind racing. I had browsed through several different sites. I couldn't believe what I had found. My favourite was an American site, 'PerfectlyThin.' Here was proof in black and white that the desire to be really thin was not a mental illness. I was right! The site was full of pages of seriously skinny girls and there were letters, stories and posts by girls who sounded just like me. That was the best part. Some girls had even made up collages of pictures of ideal bodies for 'Thinspiration.' I quickly discovered that the term 'pro-ana' referred to a movement that received a lot of bad publicity, but this site was clearly not bad at all. For the first time in ages I felt understood and I had found people I could relate to. I couldn't wait to join the discussions. The only downside was the girls in the pictures were so thin that I realised how big I actually was. It would be good to find a UK site, so I clicked on 'contact' and emailed the organiser, asking whether there were any sites based near me in England. I listed my age and address and just signed it as 'Leila.' It would be great to get a response, but for now I was just happy to know that there were others out there like me.

On Tuesday evening I came home straight after school. Mum had said she would be out that evening as she was visiting a friend and taking Lily with her, so the rest of us would have to make our own dinner. For once I could eat at home as I knew the house would be empty. Dad would be at work till late and Jenna was going over to Mary's for the evening.

I rushed home from school to prepare my food. I found myself thinking a lot about my mealtimes and it was getting hard to concentrate on anything else. Each meal was preceded by a huge amount of anxiety as so much could go wrong and stop me having the correct amount of food. I'd thrown a huge strop earlier in the week, when Mum had forgotten to buy tomatoes and Jenna had looked at me as if I were insane. I couldn't explain why it was so important; it was a bit like my twitches, it had to be done correctly or my fears would be realised. In this case I would start putting on weight instead of losing it and completely lose control; that thought sent chills up and down my spine.

I let myself into the house, dropped my bag in the hall and went straight to the kitchen. The house was eerily silent, save for the humming of the electrical appliances, and the ticking of the clock in the hall. I washed the salad vegetables and made a huge plate of lettuce, tomatoes and spring onions. It was still early, but the earlier I ate the less time I would have to worry about my meal, and the more time I would have for exercise later. As I put the remaining tomatoes back in the fridge, I spotted half a huge creamy gateau that Mum had made the day before. She'd seemed a bit put out that I hadn't wanted any, but I had made out that I was feeling sick after eating too much at McDonald's. The very word made me shudder – I wouldn't put McDonald's greasy junk food anywhere near my mouth now – that really would make me feel nauseous.

I carefully slid the cake out of the fridge, just to get a closer look at it. Although I no longer allowed such sweet foods into my body, I was increasingly fascinated by food, even surprising my food tech teacher with my sudden interest in nutrition lessons. Despite the thoughts running through my head, I heard my stomach rumble. I so rarely felt hungry these days, but all of a sudden the sight of the cake had got my tastes buds going and before I even realised what I was doing, I was shoving the cake into my mouth with my hands, eating it as fast as I could. I closed my eyes and savoured the taste in my mouth; I'd forgotten how heavenly Mum's cake was. As I was licking the plate clean, desperate to get every last morsel inside me, I caught sight of my reflection in the window and realised with horror what I'd done. I knew that Mum cared nothing about calories and would have poured cream, butter and sugar into the cake; after all I'd helped her make it countless times in the past.

I got up and rushed out of the room and up the stairs taking them two at a time. My heart was racing and I could feel myself getting hotter and hotter. I had to get the food out of me before it had a chance to settle as fat on my body. I locked myself into the bathroom I shared with Jenna and lifted the toilet seat. I put two fingers down my throat and pressed. After a couple of gags, with tears streaming out of my eyes, I vomited out the cake. I kept going until I could see only dark liquid, the coffee I'd had earlier, at which point it seemed safe to stop. I washed my face with cold water and brushed my teeth, then scrubbed the toilet thoroughly, shivering at the hideousness of it all. My throat was scratched and raw, and I felt weak from the sudden exertion, yet elated at the same time. I went back down to the kitchen, remembering the plate of salad sitting on the kitchen counter. The sight of it revolted me now; how could I have been going to eat as much as that? The portion size was ridiculous. I swept the food into a carrier bag and buried it in the bin. Mum wasn't in the habit of going through the bins as far as I knew. Momentarily I panicked about the cake, but the perfect solution quickly came to me; I would say Samia and Cherry had come home from school with me and the three of us had polished it off. Mum would like that. I could always make her a replacement if necessary.

Upstairs in my room I lay down on my bed, exhausted. I was terrified by what had just happened. My iron will had snapped and I had felt hungry. How greedy could I get? No wonder I was still fat. The purging had, however, made me feel thoroughly cleansed and light, free of food inside my body, but also somehow rid of all the badness inside me. It felt great. I would allow myself a little lie down after my DVD workout, if I still felt tired. I put the disc in the machine and set to work. I would concentrate on my thighs today, maybe do the routine twice. I smiled. Three times even. I was back in control again.

10

JENNA

A few weeks after Leila and I had had our chat, Mum and Leila had a furious row. Everybody was home at the same time for once. Dad got home from work at about six, which is pretty unusual for him, Leila was upstairs and Lily and I were watching TV. Mum was in the kitchen, making a lasagne and salad for dinner. The smell coming from the kitchen was heavenly and I was looking forward to dinner. Mum went to the bottom of the stairs.

'Leila' she called up. 'Can you come down here a minute?'

I heard Leila open the bedroom door and come to the top of the stairs.

'What is it Mum? I'm busy.'

'I want you to come down here now.'

Mum popped her head into the living room. 'Jenna, tell everyone dinner's ready.'

I went and got Dad and he joined Lily and I at the table.

There was a strange atmosphere but I couldn't put my finger on what was causing it. Leila came in looking cross, followed by Mum.

'Why have you got me down here Mum?' she asked. 'I'm

in the middle of a history essay.'

Mum folded her arms. 'Because it's dinner time' she said. 'Sit down at the table; we're having dinner together as a family. It's the first time we've all been home together for ages and I'm fed up with all of us being in and out at different times. I've cooked your favourite meal, its lasagne. And there's plenty of salad,' she stressed.

'I've already eaten' said Leila sullenly. I noticed how uncomfortable she looked. Looking at her face more closely, I realised with shock that she'd lost a lot of weight. 'I'm not hungry' she persisted.

'Sit. Down. Now.' Mum's words and harsh tone made us all jump. Mum rarely raised her voice but when she did it had an immediate effect.

Leila sat down, folded her arms and glowered at the table.

'Well, this is nice' said Dad, attempting to lighten the mood.

Lily had brought her latest Sindy doll to the table and was arranging her clothes, oblivious to what was going on around her.

'Put that down, Lily' snapped Mum 'and get on with your meal.'

Lily pouted and kicked at the table leg as Mum put the lasagne and salad bowls in the middle of the table and everyone helped themselves. Leila put a small amount of salad on her plate.

'Have some lasagne, Leila' said Mum.

'I told you, Mum, I've already eaten.'

'What exactly did you eat and where?' asked Mum.

I looked down at my plate, uncomfortable.

'Well? I'm waiting.'

'God, you sound like a teacher.'

'Leila' warned Dad

Leila glared at him. 'Well she does. I had a burger and chips with Samia after school.'

'So if I ring Samia to confirm this, she will tell me exactly the same?'

'Don't you dare!' shouted Leila. 'You have no right to hassle my friends.'

I was watching Leila closely and despite her fury I could read something else on her face. When Mum had mentioned ringing Samia she had looked really alarmed. I also realised that whilst this row was going on nobody was eating anything. Dad must have been thinking along the same lines. 'Let's get on with our dinner' he said.

I started eating my lasagne but the argument had taken away some of my appetite. Out of the corner of my eye I could see Leila poking at her salad. She was eating a little of it, but mostly pushing it around her plate.

She suddenly rounded on me. 'Are you watching me?' she asked.

I was shocked at her tone of voice. Mum stood up.

'I've had enough of this charade' she said. 'You don't speak to your sister like that and you are going to stay at the table until I've seen you finish that lasagne. You've lost far too much weight lately and I don't think you're eating properly. There'll be no more of this eating out with Samia nonsense, until I see an improvement. I expect you home for dinner every night from now on.'

Leila jumped up from the table. 'How dare you?' she shouted. 'How can I eat when you're making such a drama out of everything and everyone is watching me? You're just trying to make me fat and it won't work.'

With that she ran out of the room and up the stairs, leaving us all a in a state of shock.

Mum sat down, looking defeated. She looked at Dad. 'I was right.' she said. Dad looked at me.

'Jenna, take Lily into the other room.'

As Lily and I went out of the room I could hear Mum and Dad continuing the conversation. Lily ran off into the living room but I hovered outside the kitchen door, trying to catch what they were saying. I could understand them not wanting Lily to hear, but I was old enough to know what was going on.

'We do have a problem, William.' Mum said.

'You're right, darling. I'm sorry I doubted you. I knew she'd lost weight but now I've seen how resistant she is to eating …' his voice trailed off and I heard the chair scrape against the kitchen floor as he stood up from the table. 'I'll go and talk to her' he said, 'see if I can get through to her.'

At that moment Lily must have switched the TV on as music blared out from the living room drowning out the conversation, but not before I'd heard Dad say, 'She's like a different person lately, Jean.'

I quickly went into the living room and threw myself onto the sofa with Lily. She snuggled up to me and I held her tight. I was feeling so sad. Dad was right; she was turning into a different person. What was happening to my sister? That evening something that I didn't want to acknowledge had become unavoidably clear to me. Leila was anorexic.

The Voice

The girl was succumbing. The Voice's spell had been cast and the girl was easy prey. As long as she continued to listen and withstood the outsiders, there would be no danger of her escaping. The Voice whispered a little louder.

11

LEILA

I rushed upstairs, fell onto my bed and pounded the pillow with my fists. I was absolutely furious. How dare Mum embarrass me like that, making the whole family watch me eat? How dare she? Also eating away at me was the fact that I'd had some extra calories that I hadn't planned on. I'd have to do some more exercise and make up for it by eating less tomorrow. At least I hadn't been forced to eat any of the lasagne. I shuddered at the thought. And what if Mum rang Samia? She couldn't make me eat at home, could she? The absolute control I had over everything was being threatened and I could feel myself falling apart.

There was a knock at the door.
'Go away' I said, into the pillow.
The door opened and Dad stuck his head around it.
'It's me' he said. 'Can I come in?'
I sat up and wiped my face.
'I suppose so' I said, maybe Dad would be able to talk some sense into Mum. Dad came over and sat down on the bed.

'What are we going to do with you?' he said.

'There's nothing wrong with me, Dad' I wailed. 'It's just Mum making a big fuss as usual. Can't you get her off my back?'

Dad looked at me for a moment.

'Your mother isn't making a fuss' he began, holding his hand up when I started to protest.

'Hear me out first' he said, 'then you can say your bit.'

He took a deep breath.

'Your mum and I have noticed that you have lost weight lately. I know you wanted to lose a bit of weight, but we think you've taken it too far. You're looking too thin now and very pale. And you don't seem your old self. I've noticed you snapping a lot lately and that isn't like you. How could you snap at your old Dad, eh?'

I managed a smile.

'What happened this evening was actually down to me. I thought Mum was maybe over worried, so I suggested we get you down for dinner and you could prove that there was nothing wrong. But you have to admit Leila, the way it turned out was clear for us all to see. Even Jenna noticed. I am really worried now. That wasn't a normal reaction you had there. You seemed really frightened about eating. Is that true? Are you afraid to eat?'

I was weighing up the possibilities in my mind. I realised I could do a deal with Dad and maybe get Mum off my case.

'I'm sorry Dad,' I began. 'I've got so used to my new healthy regime and choosing the correct combination of foods, that Mum hauling me down to dinner like that threw me off course.' I looked at him. 'I did lie. I didn't eat chips with Samia, but I did have a sandwich when I got in from school before everyone came home.' My mind was working nineteen to the dozen and I chose my words carefully. 'I do have a problem and I know it's a bit odd.' I took a deep breath and looked at my hands. 'I don't like eating in front of other people.'

'Is that what tonight was all about?' Dad asked.

I nodded, hating myself for lying but I had no choice. 'I will try and do something about it, Dad, but Mum getting on at me just makes it worse.'

Dad nodded. 'Ok' he said 'I'll see what I can do.' He ruffled my hair. 'Try and be a bit nicer' he added, 'it makes my life easier too, you know.'

'Sure, Dad' I said, breathing a sigh of relief.

It felt weird, lying to Dad. Just for a second I questioned what I was doing, but as soon as I started to doubt myself, a buzzing started up in my head. The Voice again. It rarely left me in peace these days.

Be very careful listening to other people, they're trying to make you fat.

I tried to shut it out. The buzzing intensified.

They don't understand how good it feels to be thin. Are you really happy to be this size?

I ran my hands over my waist. I pinched a lump of fat between my fingers. Gross.

Exactly! It's a trick. You can't trust anyone. You did well, getting your Dad on your side.

Surely my parents were only doing what they think is best?

Samia's thinner than you. Cherry's thinner than you. Do I need to go on?

Maybe The Voice was right. As I gazed up at the ceiling I sensed a presence over by the window. The shadow from the other night was back. It was in exactly the same place, but it was different this time. It had more of a shape now, like a real person. I glanced behind me but there was no one there.

Do you see that? It's getting bigger. That's what will happen to you if you don't listen to me.

I looked frantically around the room. Surely there must be a rational explanation for this shadow? There was nothing in the path of the streetlight.

There's nothing there. You know that, don't you?

Curiously I felt calmer. I did know. I was wrong to question The Voice. The shadow flickered, then disappeared. My head was quiet. I had to work harder. If it meant isolating myself from other people, then bring it on. I would do whatever it took to keep the weight off and The Voice out of my head.

I got up, locked the door and put on my exercise DVD. I would need to spend at least an extra forty minutes on my workout tonight, thanks to Mum. As I jumped up and down I realised that I had managed to avert a catastrophe, but for how long could I keep everyone at bay?

12

JENNA

I went to bed early that night and pretended to be asleep when Leila came up. She'd hurt me the way she'd spoken to me earlier and the realisation that she was ill had upset me. Typically, for once I couldn't sleep and had to lie really still when she came up and went through her whole bedroom rigmarole of touching the walls. Although I had to admit that since she had become more focused on her diet, she was much better with her twitches. I'd watched a TV documentary once which explained that people often transferred one type of addictive behaviour to another. Leila seemed to be replacing her original obsession with dieting. Why couldn't she just be normal? I had to keep reminding myself that she wasn't well. I'd go and do some research on eating disorders tomorrow, maybe go to the library to get out of the house, and see if I could find out how best to help her. I might try and talk to Charlie about it too, as he looked at things in such a different way. The room went completely dark as Leila turned her bedside lamp out and we both followed our separate, lonely, paths to an uneasy sleep.

School was particularly hideous the next day. Wednesday was always the worst day of the week, double PE with Miss Hayden in her chavvy tracksuit. Today she'd had us all running round the muddy school field doing cross country. This is hardly the country! Why didn't they admit what it really was, an attempt to make teenage girls look as undignified as possible? Of course it meant I came home sweaty and muddy as there was no way any of us would use the manky school showers. I don't do public showers; it was a private cubicle or nothing for me. I was looking forward to this evening for another reason as well. Dad was taking Lily to her tap class and Leila was babysitting for our aunt, so I would have Mum all to myself. That meant a hassle free evening with no arguments, no raised voices, and best of all we could eat a meal together in peace and enjoy it, without the hideous tension that normally reigned over the table. Mum was trying not to put pressure on Leila, but I was sure she would be changing her tactics soon as Leila was getting worse. She barely spoke to any of us any more and was definitely still losing weight. Mum had also lost weight lately, I'd realised with a shock the other day. That was down to Leila too, as I know Mum's been worrying herself sick. That girl has so much to answer for.

I felt one hundred per cent better when I came out of the shower, smelling more like a grapefruit than an old sock thanks to the wickedly smelly shower gel Mary had given me for Christmas. I went straight down to the kitchen, where Mum was washing some salad. 'I hope you've got something seriously calorie laden to go with that Mum' I teased, 'we've got the run of the kitchen tonight, don't forget?'

'You better believe it darling' she said, 'I've made some very cheesy mushroomy pizza to go with this salad, with ice cream to follow. How does that sound?'

I gave her a big hug and a squeeze. 'Fantastic' I said. 'Shall I choose us a DVD to watch?'

That was another treat. Cbeebies was normally the only channel allowed on the TV when Lily was around.

I picked out 'Twilight' to watch as I hadn't gotten around to seeing it yet. I knew Mum wouldn't mind as she wanted to know what all the fuss was about. I thought it would probably be a bit cheesy but I couldn't wait to see Jacob the Werewolf. He is gorgeous. All my friends prefer Edward Cullen of course but I can't take him seriously. He pales into uninteresting insignificance next to Jacob who is far more alluring. My friends and I have long discussions about this and even managed to get chucked out of the school library one lunch time for making too much noise. Miss Leslie refused to believe we were discussing books; Mary argued until she was blue in the face but the Librarian wouldn't back down.

We had been watching the film for half an hour and I was getting a bit sick of the meaningful looks which Edward was giving Bella (they were supposed to mean he was 'being a Vampire' but to me looked a bit like he was slightly constipated) when Mum's mobile started to ring.

'Don't answer it Mum' I said. 'You'll miss the film.' She gave me an apologetic look whilst reaching for the phone. I sighed and picked up the remote to pause the video.

'It's an unknown number' she said distractedly, as she pressed the button to listen.

'Yes' she said. 'This is Mrs Summers. No, not at all, this is a perfect time to talk,' she said, mouthing 'sorry' to me. I had no idea who was on the phone and was prevented from eavesdropping when she got up and took the phone into the kitchen and shut the door behind her. That told me, I thought, feeling miffed. Well there was no way I was going to miss the film, so I pressed play and quickly got engrossed as Jacob made his entrance and I forgot that Mum wasn't even there.

She must have been on the phone for ages because she missed practically the whole of the film. She motioned to me not to stop it when she came back so I had to wait until the film was over before I could ask her what had happened. I could see she looked anxious and my heart sank.

'Who was that on the phone?' I asked. 'You were gone for ages.'

'It was Mrs Paris, she wanted to talk to me about Leila.'

'Mrs Paris?' I was shocked. She was Leila's Head of Year and was seriously scary. My head was buzzing with questions as a teacher had never rung home before. Mum sighed.

'The school are worried about Leila. They've noticed she hasn't been looking very well lately. To be honest, I was expecting something like this. I've made an appointment to go in and see Mrs Paris next week. I'd prefer it if you didn't mention this to Leila – there's no need to worry her in advance.'

At that moment the noise of the key turning in the front door sounded and Lily came bounding into the living room, followed by a somewhat harried looking Dad. Our discussion was clearly over. I got up and took the DVD out and put it away, then went off upstairs to get some peace and quiet, as Lily launched into a breathless account of her evening.

13

LEILA

As soon as I got out of school at the end of the day I changed into my trainers, hitched my bag onto my back and ran down to the park. It backed onto my garden so it was really close to home. I often met Samia there after school, just to hang out and chat on the swings. The park had an old shelter too which felt more private; the little kids didn't bother us there. I had texted Samia to wait for me; she'd have Cherry for company anyway. I had neglected them a bit lately as I'd been feeling so antisocial and I wanted to make up for it by spending some time with them.

As I approached the playground I wondered whether 'PerfectlyThin' had replied to my email yet. I had been checking every day but was disappointed so far. I stopped to light a cigarette and inhaled deeply. My friends didn't like me smoking, so I tried to do it out of their sight. I could see that they weren't in the shelter, so carried on down to the swings. I saw Cherry's mane of gorgeous dark red curls straight away, but then did a double take. I couldn't see Samia, but two other girls were there and I could have sworn that one of them was Kelsey Atwood. It was bad enough that she'd turned up at the detention the other night. What on earth was she doing here?

I soon realised that Kelsey's companion was Lizzie Grimshaw, a nasty piece of work from our class. I think most people found Kelsey odd and a little sinister, but it was hard to pinpoint what exactly it was that was disturbing about her. Her dark Gothic image didn't help. She was an unlikely companion for Lizzie who was a complete airhead, with a permanent orange tan and trashy dress sense. Today she was wearing an extremely high pair of shoes.

I took a deep breath and carried on towards them. I wasn't in the best of moods as it was after last night's row with Mum, and could have done without any aggro from Kelsey and Lizzie. Lizzie was fixing her lipstick and as she saw me approaching she nudged Kelsey and put her compact into her bag. I threw away my cigarette and went to meet them. Thankfully I noticed that Samia was there. She had been obscured by Kelsey's big stocky body. Kelsey had wedged her large backside into a swing seat meant for a much younger person. She could do with a few diet tips. Lizzie nonchalantly gave her a push and they both stared as I approached.

'Hi' I said.

Cherry gave me a big smile, but Samia looked fed up. Lizzie turned slowly round. 'So this is where you guys hang out. We thought we'd come along and see what you get up to after school. I'm disappointed though – where's all the talent?'

I ignored her. Typical Lizzie, her whole world revolved around boys.

'I suppose it's on your way home isn't it, you live close to the park don't you Leila?' Lizzie persisted. 'It looks a bit posh around here.'

'Hardly' I shrugged. 'Thanks for waiting Sam,' I wanted to tell Samia about my detention but I didn't particularly want to discuss it in front of Kelsey and Lizzie. I needn't have worried. Lizzie suddenly stopped the swing she was pushing by catching hold of the chain. Clearly she had a very short attention span. She raised her eyebrows at Kelsey.

'Come on Kelsey' she said. 'This is boring. Let's go down the Town – you never know there might be a riot or something interesting going on.' With that she turned and stomped off across the grass, with Kelsey hurrying to keep up with her.

'Thank God for that!' said Samia. 'I thought they'd be here all night! I wonder why they wanted to come here with us?'

I told the others about my detention and how Kelsey had tried to walk home with me. 'She gives me the creeps.'

'She is strange' Samia agreed. 'She's always banging on about how Larksmead is a better school than Stenfield Academy and how she should have gone there. I don't know why she thinks it's so great.'

Cherry frowned. 'I think she might be lonely and hides behind that Goth appearance. Lizzie is her only friend at our school – that says it all really. She puts on an act like she doesn't care, but I think she does. I think she's quite mixed up.' Cherry was usually good at sussing people out.

'Well her social skills are definitely lacking.' I snorted. 'And hanging round with Lizzie won't endear her to anybody.'

Cherry interjected. 'Look, they've gone now, so why are we wasting our time talking about them?' She looked at her watch. 'And speaking of time I need to start heading back now anyway. Alfie needs baby sitting as Mum is working tonight. Are you two coming?' Samia and I walked Cherry over to the far side of the park and waited with her until her bus came.

'Have you lost more weight?' asked Samia.

I hope so 'Not as far as I know.'

'Your face looks thinner. Actually, you look knackered. Don't overdo it.'

'Don't be stupid' I said sharply. Samia looked surprised.

'Why do you keep snapping at me? I'm your friend, re-member?'

'Sorry. I am a bit tired today. I'll try and get to bed earlier tonight.'

I watched Samia as she walked off in the opposite di-rection. She looked a bit downcast and I resolved to try and be less irritable with my friends. I took my time walking home, not looking forward to another lecture from Mum.

I let myself into the house quietly, hoping Mum hadn't heard me, and I was relieved when I realised that Mum and Lily hadn't got home yet and Jenna was nowhere to be seen. I went into the kitchen and took out a plate and some cutlery. I checked to see what was in the fridge. There was a selection of cheeses which I took out and found half a loaf of bread on the kitchen counter. I hacked off a thin slice of bread, deliberately scattering some crumbs on the work surface, then put the plate, cutlery and bread knife into the washing up bowl. I poured some water over them and added some washing up liquid, creating a bowl full of frothy bubbles. I left the crumbs on the counter. The mess would drive Mum mad, but at least she would believe that I had eaten a sandwich when she came in.

I dried my hands quickly and was about to go upstairs when I heard Mum and Lily at the front door. I made for the stairs quickly, hoping to avoid them, but just as I had put my foot delicately on the bottom stair, Mum's bionic ears must have vibrated, as she called out 'Lee is that you love? Do you want some tea?'

'No, thanks Mum' I said. 'I'm going upstairs to do my homework.' I waited for Mum to start nagging me about food, but nothing happened. Dad must have had a word with her asking her to lay off me for a bit. I wondered whether Jenna was still being a bit off with me after last night, but I knew she'd soon come round. I hadn't eaten since breakfast and was feeling very virtuous. I didn't even feel hungry. I ran up the stairs and got out my laptop. Samia's comments were on my mind. I really needed to connect with people online who were on the same wavelength.

I logged in and went straight to my email account. I had two messages and one of them was from PerfectlyThin! I couldn't open it quickly enough – my hands were actually trembling. The reply was really friendly and gave me a link to a group that was active in my area. I couldn't believe my luck.

The first thing I needed to do was to register on the site, so that I could make contact with other people. I thought for a bit about what to call myself but decided on my own name. I had nothing to hide, and after all I hoped to make some friends. There were lots of flashing messages before I actually registered, ensuring that I knew what I was letting myself in for and I clicked my way through without actually reading them – who does? I added a few details to my profile then logged into the forum and clicked on the newcomers page for my area.

I had only been logged on for a few minutes when replies started coming into my messages. This must be why Jenna enjoyed Facebook so much. I'd never had much time for it but now that I was reaching out to people I loved the speed at which things could happen. A request to chat popped up on the screen, from somebody called Kate. Why not, I thought, and clicked to go into the chat room. There were two other girls in there, RosieB and Princessgirl.

Kate: Hi Leila
RosieB: Welcome
Princessgirl: Yeah hi
Leila: Hello
RosieB: A new girl at last!! It's been ages. I think people are scared
Princessgirl: But we don't bite!
RosieB: Especially not food
Kate: LOL
RosieB: Where do you live?
Leila: Stenfield. Do you know it?
Kate: No way! I'm not that far from there in Munstown.
RosieB: Me too
Princessgirl: I live much further out but this is the nearest group.
RosieB: Have you joined any other sites?
Leila: No
RosieB: You're not the new girl anymore Kate.
Princessgirl: Kate joined weeks ago. I have to go now. See you all. Chat to you more next time Leila. Stay thin
RosieB: I'm off too. Time to do battle with my dad again. Stay thin
Kate: Are you ok Leila?
Leila: Nervous! It's my first time on the site
Kate: Don't be nervous, it's cool here. Everything we say is

completely private. I've met loads of great people who understand me. How old are you?

    Leila: Fifteen, nearly sixteen.

    Kate: I'm fourteen, Year 9. Are you Ana or Mia?

    Leila:???

    Kate: Anorexic or Bulimic

    Leila: I'm on a diet cos I'm too fat. No labels

    Kate: Me too. I don't binge; just eat as little as I can. I weigh 95 pounds at the moment but I'm nowhere near my target yet. This site has some great tips to lose weight on it, have you had a look?

    Leila: No! I'm gonna have a look now before it gets too late

    Kate: Shame. Come back soon - I'm here every evening. Speak soon?

    Leila: Yeah

I signed off, suddenly alarmed at what I was doing. I was exhilarated and scared at the same time. I didn't know these girls, but they understood me so deep down I thought they were ok. We spoke the same language. Part of me wanted to log back on and try and find Kate again, but I had felt stupid not knowing what she was talking about at first. I wanted to get a hang of the site and the jargon before I went on again. One thing was for sure, wild horses wouldn't keep me out of that chat room tomorrow.

I put the laptop on pause and resolved to go back to it after I had done some exercise. If Kate weighed ninety-five pounds then she would think I was gross. I wondered how much the others weighed. Checking out the Internet had been well worth it, now I had a new incentive. My new friends would appreciate the effort I was putting into looking good even if no one else did. As the music started I felt relief wash over me. I'd made it through another day, but best of all I was no longer alone.

The Voice

The girl could hear The Voice clearly now:
'Mirror, mirror on the wall,
Who is the thinnest of them all?'

14

JENNA

I was heading off for the library on Saturday morning when I heard footsteps running down the road after me. It was Charlie. We'd quickly become friends after the first evening when we watched a DVD together, I had to keep pinching myself to be sure it was true.

'I was just coming round to see what you were up to,' he gasped, catching his breath. 'Where are you going?'

'I'm off to the town library.' I told him. 'There's some stuff I need to look up.'

'What, for school?' he asked. I could have pretended it was for homework but I needed to talk to someone.

'No.' I admitted. I felt a bit unsure what to say next. 'It's complicated' I said.

Charlie thought for a minute. 'Tell you what. How about we go to Café Blanco first and you can tell me all about it. If you want to, I mean?' he added, cautiously. 'Then we can go to the library.'

Café Blanco was a great café in the centre of town, where loads of teenagers hung out. We walked along the road in a companionable silence, Charlie's use of the word 'we' was ringing happily in my ears. That's what I liked about Charlie. He was a bit of a dreamer, like me, and I didn't mind when he was being quiet. Neither of us felt the need to fill in the gaps with nonsense. Once we were sat down with our hot chocolates I told him about the row at home last night and how I was worried that Leila was anorexic. Charlie listened without interrupting.

'This is probably going to surprise you,' he said, 'but I had already guessed that Leila had problems. There was that time when my mum offered her an ice cream, do you remember? I thought she looked really uncomfortable. And, well, she has that haunted look in her eyes, which I recognised.'

'What do you mean, recognised?' I asked.

'I recognise that gaunt, haunted expression. My step sister Molly was anorexic a few years ago. She's a lot better now, although I'm not sure she'll ever be exactly how she was before. She's Dad's daughter, from his first marriage. She used to live with us and got ill when she was about twelve. I was only about Lily's age then, so I didn't really know what was going on. But as I got older, I couldn't help but be drawn into it. Things got so bad between Mum and Dad; I used to lie awake at night, worrying they were going to break up. Then Molly went into hospital and when she came out she went to live with her real Mum. She was in and out of hospital for a few years, but the last year or two she's been a lot better. She's really trying hard and is going to college now, catching up on the studies she missed. When I saw Leila, she had exactly the same expression on her face as Molly had. Big dark eyes, in a pale, gaunt face.... Molly doesn't look like that anymore and I'm sure Leila won't either one day, but it's very hard. I do understand how you feel though. We all wanted to make her better, but there was nothing we could do about it until she wanted to get better herself. I don't think Leila is aware she has a problem, is she?'

I shook my head.

Charlie got up and stretched his legs. 'How about I come to the library with you and we can see what we can find out? Then I'll get you a McDonald's and we can do some serious eating. Someone around here has to.'

I smiled and got up. I was so pleased I'd told Charlie, it really helped to share what was going on with a friend and I loved how he'd tried to help his sister. We headed off to the library; I knew we wouldn't find any real answers there, but if felt good to be doing something and even better to have someone to share it with.

Charlie and I had spent the rest of the morning at the Town Library. It had only recently reopened and was housed in a brand new modern building, with lots of glass. There were several different zones in the new library. Mum said when she was younger there had been a separate Children's department with dedicated staff to help you, but nowadays with all the Library cutbacks the few staff that were left were based in the adult library and looked suspiciously at any teenagers hanging around in the adult section. I was at the kind of cross over age anyway and today the information we were looking for was in the adult section, but I always felt a bit out of place there, much preferring the bright and colourful atmosphere of the picture books and posters in the adjacent room. There was a new teen zone upstairs, but whenever I had ventured up there it was always full and I wasn't confident enough to sit on my own amongst a crowd of people. However, I wasn't on my own today and I couldn't help smiling to myself at that thought; being with Charlie was making me feel much more confident in facing the world.

First of all we managed to get a slot on the Internet for half an hour and did some research online. There's so much information out there that I didn't really know where to start. Charlie told me about some of the Pro-Ana sites which had sprung up where sufferers encourage one another to lose weight and actually boast online about how skinny they are. It was really sickening. I thought we should start a campaign to get them shut down, but Charlie said we'd be better conserving our energy with our current battle, to save my sister. All in all it was pretty depressing stuff. A lot of boys are increasingly affected too, which surprised me. After the Internet session, I went and browsed amongst the bookshelves and found a couple of books which looked quite helpful and informative. I was going to hide them from Leila though; I didn't want her to think I was ganging up on her too.

We had lunch in McDonald's and I couldn't help feeling a bit pleased that a group of girls from my year were in there and I noticed them looking appreciatively at Charlie. I was so pleased he'd picked me as a friend. I felt as if I'd known him for ages. In the end he didn't eat much, as he had to go to his Gym Club that afternoon, but he went out of his way to assure me that he wasn't on a diet; aware I'd just been reading about how many boys develop anorexia nowadays. I wasn't worried; I could totally understand that he wouldn't want to be doing backflips with a Quarter pounder, double fries and milkshake sloshing around in his stomach.

I was wondering what to do with myself that afternoon as I had no plans. Mary had gone to her Grandma's in Somerset, so was away for the whole weekend. Charlie had got up to leave and was rummaging around in his bag.

'What are you doing this afternoon?' he asked

'Nothing' I said. He must think I was really boring.

'Why don't you come along?'

'To gymnastics?'

'Obviously' he laughed. 'You said you like watching sport.'

I was amazed he'd remembered that.

'Why not?' I said, trying my best to look cool and composed.

The club took place in the sports hall at Larksmead, which gave me a chance to nosey around the school to see what it was like. I spent the next two hours watching the club members practice their floor, bar and beam routines; they had a competition coming up. Charlie was fantastic, of course and naturally I teased him for running around in a leotard, but I was secretly really proud of him and thought he looked great in it. It was a fun afternoon, especially as one of my friends from school was there, as her younger sister was in the club, so we sat and chatted as we watched. It was good to relax and enjoy myself, away from all the troubles at home. I couldn't help noticing the different shapes and sizes of the gymnasts, particularly the girls. They looked confident; like they were taking part in the sport because they enjoyed it, not to punish and reduce their bodies, like Leila did with her mad exercise routine. Already I'd gathered from my research in the library that addiction to exercise is a symptom of anorexia. I shook my head. I'd realised I was thinking about Leila again and switched my attention back to watching the acrobatics in front of me. I was determined that nothing was going to get in the way of me enjoying this day, which had turned out to be the most fun I'd had in a long time.

15

LEILA

I had arranged to meet Samia and Cherry at Café Blanco in town on Saturday morning. The large but cosy coffee bar was our favourite place to hang out and my friends and I quite often went there at the weekend. It got a little busy on Saturdays, with all the shoppers making the most of the day off, but there were plenty of large comfy seating areas and more often than not we managed to get one to ourselves.

I had avoided meeting up with my friends for the last couple of weeks as it usually involved some kind of food and I was getting a little jumpy around the subject. I'd had an uncomfortable conversation with Cherry the other day after PE. We were getting changed back into our uniform. I always tried to get dressed as quickly as possible; apart from being horribly self-conscious I wanted to get away from the smell of sweaty bodies which lingered in the changing rooms. Cherry was tying her hair up in the mirror, pulling her long curls into a twisted knot on the back of her head. She was watching me in the mirror.

'Are you still dieting Leila? You look thinner than you

did last week.'

'Of course not. It's these clothes. And I don't diet, I keep telling you, I just eat healthy food.'

'Whatever' she said. 'You need to be careful. Do you want to come to lunch with me? It's fish and chips today.'

'I've got to go to Maths club.'

'You can't work 24/7. I can't remember the last time we went out together, you need to lighten up.'

'I'd better go or I'll be late' I said quickly, looking at my watch. 'See you after lunch.'

I could feel her eyes following me as I went out. I wished she'd take that concerned expression off her face. It was none of her business.

I arrived at Café Blanco earlier than the appointed time and ordered myself a black filter coffee and a large glass of iced water with a straw. Luckily, my favourite corner of the cafe by the window was free, so I could watch the world go by as I waited for my friends. About ten minutes later Samia and Cherry came in together, smiling and waving as they spotted me in the window. I couldn't help but notice what good looking girls they were, both were wearing jeans; Samia's were black teamed with high platform boots and a white long sleeved top, Cherry's were blue; she wore flat pink pumps and a black t-shirt. They were tall girls, and really made quite an impression, with their denim clad legs that went on forever. I looked down at my thighs and pinched them angrily under the table. Despite my drastic regime I didn't seem to be getting anywhere near as slim as my friends. I'd have to try harder.

The girls came over to me before they went to order. Samia sat down on the sofa next to me and Cherry put her bag on the chair opposite us.

'Hi Lee' she said. 'Can I get you anything else?'

I smiled, flinching inside. 'No thanks I'm fine with this' I said. Minutes later Cherry came back with a tray laden with caramel Frappuccinos topped with cream and two large slices of cake.

'You can help us with this lot!' said Cherry. 'I've been looking forward to this ever since we arranged to meet yesterday.' She picked up a fork and was in the process of putting the first forkful into her mouth when she froze, her eyes fixed on the window. 'Don't look now' she said, 'but I think we are about to be ambushed.' Both Cherry and I immediately ignored her warning and turned round to look out of the window. Kelsey and Lizzie were pressing their noses up to the glass and waving at them.

'We're cornered' groaned Samia. 'I can't bear it. It's obvious we've only just arrived.'

By this time Kelsey and Lizzie had come in and gone over to the counter. Lizzie was placing her order and they kept looking over in our direction.

'Maybe they've come in for a private conversation?' asked Cherry hopefully, but I could already see that the gruesome twosome were making their way over to our corner. I could also see that they had two drinks and three large pieces of cake on their tray; no wonder Kelsey was so large, I thought spitefully.

'Hi girls' said Lizzie brightly, as she plonked herself on the other sofa next to Cherry.

'Fancy running into you guys again. It's more fun in here than in the park anyway.' She started taking the cups and plates off of the tray. She passed a plate to Kelsey who immediately started tucking into her cake. Then to my horror she placed a plate with a large piece of chocolate cake down in front of me. 'We noticed that you hadn't got any cake so we decided to treat you to a piece, we couldn't let you sit there without eating. And actually, some of the girls in class have been saying that you're looking a bit skinny lately, but I stuck up for you, didn't I Kelsey?' she glanced at her friend, who nodded furiously, wiping crumbs from her mouth. She made me feel ill. 'I said you ate like a horse and there was nothing wrong with you, so you'd better prove me right' she said triumphantly. I pushed the plate away from me, trying not to look as horrified as I felt. Did I eat like a horse?

'No thanks' I said 'I'm full.' Inside my heart was beating so fast I was sure the others could hear it. I was furious and mortified at the same time.

'Oh go on, I'm sure you can force it down,' persisted Lizzie. 'Look how delicious it is.'

My eyes were drawn reluctantly to the cake. Dark brown frosting oozed out from the middle and all over the plate. This used to be my favourite before I started my regime. I pulled myself together; whatever was I thinking? I pushed the plate further across the table towards Kelsey. I noticed Samia glancing at Cherry, but was mostly aware that Kelsey was staring at me intently.

'You look anxious' she said, suddenly. It was the first time she had spoken. She was looking at me in that concerned way that made me feel really uncomfortable. I hated her for it. How dare she pity me?

'I'm not anxious' I said aggressively. 'I'm just not hungry. Why don't you eat the cake – you obviously enjoy it' I couldn't help adding.

'Maybe you have got a problem' said Lizzie. 'Clearly something is making you overreact.'

Suddenly I erupted. She had gone too far. The embarrassment at the situation and my fury at Lizzie and Kelsey for putting me on the spot caused me to see red. Before I could stop myself I found words angrily pouring out of my mouth.

'How dare you?' I asked 'What are you trying to do to me? I've come out with my friends to enjoy myself and you two turn up, uninvited, just like you did in the park the other day. Then you try to embarrass me! Well you're not welcome, so take your cake and go eat it somewhere else. We want to be on our own.'

Lizzie's eyes flashed angrily. 'I was only trying to be nice to you. I didn't have to buy you a cake,' she said. She looked round at the others, hoping to get some support, but Samia was looking embarrassed and Kelsey was prodding at the remnant of cake on her plate, avoiding eye contact. I felt close to tears. Cherry took control of the situation. 'I'm sorry about the cake, Lizzie' she said, 'but would you mind leaving us on our own for a bit?' She nodded at me. 'I think it might be for the best.'

Kelsey reluctantly gathered up her tray. 'Come on Lizzie' she said. 'We should go.'

Lizzie stood up and glared at me. 'I don't know what I'm going to report back to those girls now when they say that Leila doesn't eat. Maybe it's true.' She looked pointedly at me. 'You could do with fattening up a bit. Boys prefer girls with a bit of meat on them you know. You should remember that. Come on Kelsey' she added, as she moved away from the table. 'There's plenty of extra cake for us now. Laters.'

Cherry waited until Kelsey and Lizzie were well out of earshot before she spoke again. 'Are you ok Leila?' she asked. 'I know they're a pain but they were trying to be nice, weren't they? Don't you think you were a little bit rude?'

I looked furiously at Cherry. 'You think that was trying to be nice! They were trying to catch me out, more like. Lizzie is nasty and Kelsey gives me the creeps. She always seems to be looking at me. She cornered Jenna the other day and asked her questions about what I do at home. She's weird. I don't want anything to do with either of them.'

'You may be right,' Samia spoke up, 'they haven't gone about it in a very good way, but they do have a point.' She looked at Cherry questioningly. Cherry nodded. 'The thing is Lee,' she went on 'we wanted to have a chat with you today anyway. We are worried that you don't seem to eat much anymore and you're a lot quieter than you used to be and more irritable. And what they just did, well sort of proves it in a way. A few months ago you'd have eaten two pieces of that cake.'

'What are you talking about?' I said. 'You know I'm trying to eat healthily and I don't eat cake anymore. Get over it! I eat loads, just mostly at home that's all.'

'That's not what Jenna says' said Samia quietly.

'Jenna?' I exclaimed 'Have you been speaking to Jenna too? You're no better than Kelsey. How dare you question my sister? You have no right.' I was practically spitting with rage.

'Leila calm down' pleaded Cherry. 'We care about you and we've been worried about you. Healthy eating is one thing, but you don't actually look very healthy anymore. That's why we wanted to speak to you about it.'

'Well you've spoken to me now' I said, 'and I've put you straight. The only issue here is that Kelsey is annoying and I don't want to be friends with her. But if you two do, then go ahead.' I picked up my bag and stood up.

'Leila' said Cherry. 'This isn't about Kelsey. You seem to have got a bee in your bonnet about her for some reason. Lizzie is a nasty piece of work but Kelsey is just pathetic as far as I can see. It's not worth getting worked up about. Sit down, chill out.' She was trying to calm me down but her words just made me angrier. Lizzie was a bully but she barely registered on my radar. It was Kelsey who made me see red. Something about her got under my skin, big time. Samia and Cherry wouldn't understand so there was no point continuing this charade. I swung my bag defiantly over my shoulder.

'I'm going to do some shopping now. See you Monday.' I said, and with that, I was gone.

I stormed out of the cafe, incredulous at what had just happened. I should never have agreed to come out today. My friends were ganging up on me. Couldn't they see how difficult it was for me, hanging around with such tall slim people? No wonder I felt like a fat munchkin. I strode across the Marketplace heading for the shops. I was going to get some new jeans today as my old ones no longer fit me. I had been intending to ask Samia to come with me but now I was glad I hadn't. She'd probably be watching me like a hawk and I couldn't bear any more scrutiny today after that little stunt.

I spent a while browsing through the racks and picked out a pair of black skinny jeans in a size eight. I hadn't worn skinny jeans before and was quite excited about trying these on. I took a pair into the changing rooms. I pulled them on easily and did them up, but they were much too big, I must have got the wrong size. I checked the label but it confirmed that they were an eight.

I stuck my head out of the changing room and asked the assistant if she could change them for a size six. I was actually thrilled to be trying on a six but I feared they would be far too small for me. The shop had probably got the labels muddled up. The shop assistant took the original pair away and came back with the replacement. 'I think you may actually need a size four' she said, 'You're very tiny. Unfortunately we haven't got any left so I've got you the six anyway.'

I thought the woman must be mad. Size four? I hadn't realised that that size even existed. I took the new pair of jeans back into the cubicle and tried them on; I was trembling as I pulled them up – I wouldn't be able to handle it if they were too small – but they fitted well, were even slightly loose, however the words of the saleswoman were echoing in my head. I'd buy these jeans for now, but obviously I needed to get down to a size four if that was the smallest size. That explained how I could fit into a size six, it had nothing to do with my weight. I'd have to carry on with my regime for a little bit longer, until I reached my new goal. If my friends didn't like it, well maybe they weren't friends worth having, I mused as I took the jeans over to the till to pay. It wasn't such a big deal anyway; I had my friends on PerfectlyThin to talk to now.

The Voice

The girl was putty in my hands. A whisper here, a suggestion there, that was all it took to reel her in. What she needed now was a little direction...

16

JENNA

Raised voices in the kitchen greeted me when I arrived home from school today. I walked into the middle of a blazing row between Mum and Leila.

'I hate you' Leila shouted. 'How could you go behind my back like that?'

Mum looked exhausted. I'd never seen her cry, but her face was flushed and she looked as if she was close to tears.

'What's happened?' I asked.

'Mum went behind my back, that's what happened.'

'I made an appointment to see Mrs Paris today. She's worried about you Leila, it's nice of her. Besides, it's her responsibility as head of pastoral care to keep an eye on you.'

'Nice!' Disgust poured from Leila's tongue. 'It's outrageous and manipulative, that's what it is. It's none of her business, especially as there's nothing wrong with me.'

'It is her business' said Mum. 'She's head of pastoral care – looking after students is her job. She noticed that you have lost weight and your grades are down lately, that's why she wanted to speak to me.'

'Why do you keep going on about my weight? You should be pleased I'm looking after myself. I'm not going to the doctor anyway.'

'It's not up to you' Mum said. 'I've made an appointment and school have given you time off for it. We've been through this already.' Mum ran her hands through her hair, exasperated.

Leila turned to me. 'Can you believe Mum got me called out of lesson, I was dragged in front of Mrs Paris and made to talk about my diet? I wanted to die of shame. You treat me as if I'm a little kid and I'm sick of it.' She pushed her chair back, making an awful scraping noise, and flounced upstairs.

Mum sighed and sat down at the table. She rubbed her eyes.

'I'm not taking no for an answer. Maybe you could try and talk some sense into her?'

'I can try, Mum' I said, 'But it's not going to be easy.' I sat down opposite her. 'I'm glad she's going to the doctor though. I saw her getting undressed the other day and... .' I faltered, remembering the shock at how different Leila looked, the jutting ribcage visible through her vest. Tears sprung into my eyes and I wiped them away furiously. 'Mum, I wish I could do more' I wailed.

'Oh darling,' she sighed, standing up and putting her arms around me. 'It must be so hard for you, I hope you're not feeling lost in all this. Everything seems to be about Leila at the moment.'

'Typical' I managed a smile. 'Nothing new there then!' I didn't want Mum to start worrying about me as well. I stood up.

'I need to go next door. I'm babysitting Olivia for a couple of hours.'

Helen was finishing her make up in the hall mirror, looking glamorous in a blue shiny dress and heels. 'I'm glad you're here Jenna,' she said. Her hair was swept up and looked glossy. Her enviably straight hair. It was so unfair. 'I'm glad you're here to keep Charlie company. I worry that he'll forget all about Olivia.'

'There's no danger of that with me' I said, picking Olivia up out of her seat. 'You know I'll look after her. She's adorable.' I tickled her under the chin. 'Smile Olivia.'

'When she falls asleep take her upstairs to her cot' said Helen, 'I won't be out for long.'

'You look lovely' I said.

There was a loud clattering as Charlie came running down the stairs.

'Hi Jenna' he said, treating me to a huge smile which made my stomach lurch. 'I've managed to finish my homework just in time.'

'I hope you didn't rush too much Charlie.' Helen said.

'Mum. It was only Spanish. It didn't take long but I wanted to get it out of the way before the weekend. My competition is only a month away so I need to do a lot of training.'

'Charlie's trying for his silver medal, he's such a clever boy' said Helen ruffling his hair. Charlie squirmed, shaking her hand away. 'Isn't it time you went out now mum?'

'I get the message' said Helen, planting a huge kiss on Olivia's head. 'Now where did I leave my car keys?'

Moments later the front door slammed. Charlie threw himself down next to me on the sofa.

'Careful' I said 'Olivia's dropping off.' I was aware of the clock ticking loudly in the kitchen. 'It's so quiet in here. Our house is always crazy.'

'Does Lily make a lot of noise?' asked Charlie.

'Well she does…' I wasn't sure how much to say.

'Is it Leila?' he asked.

I told him all about the row she'd had with Mum.

'It's terrible, but lately I just don't enjoy being at home. There's far too much drama for my liking.'

When I got back from Charlie's I went upstairs to see Leila. I was surprised to see her sitting on the bed in her dressing gown. The bathroom door was open and the mirror was all steamed up – she'd obviously had a bath. She'd been having a lot of baths lately. They must help her relax as I hadn't seen her so composed for ages. I decided to get straight to the point; after all she knew I'd been talking to Mum.

'Are you ok?' I asked. 'Mum told me about the doctor's appointment.'

'It's no big deal' she answered. 'The doctor will see that everyone is making a fuss about nothing, then they will all have to leave me alone.'

Her answer surprised me.

'Well I hope you're right.' I was doubtful, but didn't want to antagonise her. 'Which doctor are you seeing?'

'Dr Salmon.' There was a moment's silence then we both burst out laughing.

'Dr Salmon?' I said. 'I don't envy you that.'

Leila giggled and set me off again.

'Do you remember last time we went? I couldn't look at you 'cos you made me laugh so much. It's his hair – it looks so ridiculous. Random hair sprouting around a bald spot is so not a good look. Why doesn't he just shave it off?'

'But can you imagine what he would look like completely bald?'

That set me off again. 'Stop making me laugh. Mind you I was telling Charlie what a misery you've been lately, so it's good that you're proving me wrong.'

'Is Charlie your boyfriend?' she asked.

'No! We get on really well though. Helen's nice too and as for Olivia, I just want to eat her up, she's so gorgeous.'

'I don't know what you see in babies. They cry and scream and need so much attention. I don't ever want children.'

'You'll change your mind when you're older.'

'No I won't.'

'Whatever. I want at least four children. We'll live in a big house in the country with loads of animals.'

'Well don't expect me to visit you then. A cat I could just about cope with, but that's it.'

'How did it go at the doctor's Mum?'

It was Saturday morning and I had just got up. Mum was wiping the surfaces down furiously.

'Mum?'

Mum sighed and put the dishtowel town.

'It's hard to say' she said. 'The trouble is she isn't desperately ill.'

'But she's skinny, Mum. Surely he could see that?'

'Well, yes, but he doesn't know what she looked like a few months ago. We know she's lost loads of weight rapidly but he hasn't seen her for ages. She's never ill, well…' Mum swallowed hard '… she never used to be.'

'So what did he say?'

'He weighed her, had a chat with each of us individually and said he would monitor her for the next month. He said she clearly had a healthy diet, but needed to make sure she didn't lose any more weight. A healthy diet! She pulled the wool right over his eyes.' She stopped speaking abruptly. I turned round to see Leila standing in the doorway, her green eyes glinting.

'I knew you'd twist everything! It's you who's got the problem. Have you told Jenna he said that you shouldn't hassle me and give me some trust?' She looked at me. 'Well has she?' I kept my mouth shut. 'I knew it! What he actually said was that my weight was ok and you're a liar if you say otherwise. Straight away you're disrespecting me.'

'That's enough Leila.' Mum's neck had gone pink and blotchy. I wished Leila wouldn't be so rude. 'Let's try and start over. The doctor wants you to maintain the same weight for a month. I think you'll need to eat a little more than you have been lately so that you don't lose any more weight – can you do that? Why don't you try eating with us at meal times?'

'No way, Mum. I can't.'

'And you tell me you haven't got a problem.' Shaking her head in disbelief Mum left the kitchen.

'She means well' I said.

'Oh leave me alone. I'm sick of this family.' Leila went out into the garden and slammed the back door.

I didn't see Mum for hours after that. It was best to leave her alone when she was in one of those moods. Late that afternoon she came downstairs. I was engrossed in a game on my phone.

'Can you look after Lily for a while, Jenna? I'm going next door.'

'Sure' I said absentmindedly, my attention glued to the characters jumping up and down on the screen, evading capture.

I heard Mum pull a bottle of red wine out of the rack in the kitchen that was always well stocked. I glanced up as she opened the back door and set off for next door. She had a very determined look on her face. I sincerely hoped Helen would be able to cheer her up.

17

LEILA

I had thought my head might explode after the row with Mum, how dare she go up to school and embarrass me like that? I'd had a shower, but scrubbing hard at my body didn't wash away the fury I felt inside or the self-hatred churning around in my head. I dressed in a t-shirt and a pair of shorts and sat down on the side of the bath to cut my toenails. I hated to see my legs and I looked down in disgust at my enormous thighs, blotchy and angrily red form the shower. These people who were trying to make me eat had no idea how repulsive I was. Rage welled up inside me and before I could stop myself I sliced the blade of the scissors across the fleshy part of my thigh, first one leg then the other. Bobbles of blood popped to the surface of my skin and I stared in both wonder and horror at what I had done. The stinging feeling I had felt on impact somehow felt good and I stuck the blade in again. The second cut was deeper and this time I winced at the pain but it felt good to hurt myself, this was what I deserved. A red line snaked across my thigh and drops of blood started sliding in slow motion onto the floor and made a vivid blot against the white of the floor tile. This woke me out of my reverie. Horrified, I threw the scissors into the sink, but looking down at my legs the stinging sensation and the sight of the blood made me feel calmer. I wished I could cut all the fat away. As I leant towards the sink to get a cloth I realised how light headed I was feeling and an unexpected calm had descended upon me. I would sit quietly now and try to work out my best strategy for dealing with the doctor, my parents and the school. I was in control of my body and nobody could do anything to change that. This was a battle I would win.

After a few days however, control was slipping from my grasp. As I set off for school, I charged furiously along the pavement to burn as many calories as possible, heavy drops of rain cascading down on my head, fretting about what I was going to have for lunch.

Lunchtime came around far too quickly. The Dragon Lady was watching me intently. She sat across the table from me. I stared back at her.

'What are you looking at?' I asked

'Just eat your food. I don't enjoy this anymore than you do.'

Dragon Lady was 'keeping an eye on me' at lunchtime. I was sick of her orange face and her beady eyes watching me eat. Was she trying to put me off my food? She wasn't to blame for this situation, but I hated her regardless. Luckily she was not hard to outwit and easily distracted. Noisy excited girls all around made it difficult for her to keeping a close eye on me. It could have been worse; I could have been stuck with a special needs assistant.

It was time for one of my tricks. I sat up with a jolt and imagined the shocking scene I could see behind her shoulder. She turned round to see what had caught my eye. Quick as a flash I had knocked the piece of pie onto my lap and resumed a chewing motion as she turned round.

Other days food went under the table or up my sleeve but I always had to eat some of it. I had a solution for that – they would not get the better of me by forcing me into a corner. Mrs Paris was my number one enemy for making me eat school lunches. I wanted to stick pins in her eyes.

'Can I go now? I've eaten most of it.'

'Go on then' she said. 'I still don't think you're eating enough.'

'Whatever' I said as I grabbed my bag and rushed out of the dining room. Straight up to the girls toilets where I vomited up everything that I had been forced to eat. It meant I could start afternoon lessons feeling lightheaded and virtuous. My concentration wasn't so good lately, but no wonder with all the hassle I was getting.

I'd been online last night on PerfectlyThin. I was on the site most nights; it made me irritable if I couldn't get on it. I'd started to make friends with Kate and Princessgirl. Last night we'd had a good chat.

Leila: I'm worried that I will have to see the School Nurse to be weighed. It could happen when I'm not expecting it.

Princessgirl: Say you need the bathroom on the way and load up with water. Or carry a paperweight in your pocket. That should help.

Kate: School Nurses are generally clueless. Not like the

ones in hospital. *They watch you like hawks and won't leave you alone for a minute. How's the weight going Leila?*

Leila: I've lost two stone in total. My size six jeans are way too big but I've got loads more to lose. You should see my stomach.

Princessgirl: Tell me about it. Mine is massive and as for my thighs – well imagine two elephants stuck together.

Leila: I need to do more stomach crunches before I go to bed. My mum's getting funny about me exercising and took her fitness DVD back. LOL – I know it off by heart anyway.

Kate: How's the lunchtime dragon?!!!

Leila: It's not funny. I might skip lunch next week. What can they do? Really? Not a lot.

I'd signed off after that feeling a lot more positive. The PerfectlyThin girls knew exactly what I was talking about. That night when I got in from school Mum and Lily were in the kitchen. Lily usually ate on her own when she got home from school as she went to bed so much earlier than the rest of us. Tonight Mum had made her beans on toast, normally one of Lily's favourites, but this evening she was making a fuss. She looked tired and kept grinding her fists into her eyes. Mum was clearly getting increasingly impatient.

'Come on Lily, love' she coaxed. 'Just have a few more mouthfuls.' Lily wailed loudly and put down her knife and fork. On seeing me she stretched her arms out.

'Leila' she said 'Storytime.'

'You're not having any stories until you finish your meal' said Mum.

'Leila doesn't eat' Lily announced triumphantly. 'I don't want to eat either.' She stood up and ran into the other room. Mum threw the tea towel she was holding onto the table top.

'I've just about had enough' she said. 'See what kind of

an impression you are making on your little sister? Now she thinks it's alright not to eat!' She glared at me and I recoiled at the venom in her face. 'I've had enough of this' she said. 'I'm giving you something to eat and you will eat it now.' She opened the fridge and took out a slice of quiche on a plate and slammed it down in front of me. 'Eat that' she said.

Mum is really scary when she's angry and she rarely shouted. I was caught off my guard. I didn't like to admit also that the sight of Lily's meal had – just for a nanosecond – made me feel ravenous. I was trying to deal with those terrifying feelings and now I was faced with a piece of Mum's homemade quiche. It had been one of my favourites in my previous life. I weighed up my options. I had no choice. I'd eat it, then throw it up. No way was she going to get one over on me. She was no better than a bully.

Half an hour later I had escaped upstairs and I wasted no time in emptying my stomach. As ever, the relief and feeling of emptiness was wonderful. In fact I was so busy wallowing in the relief that I barely noticed Mum had come into the room until it was too late. She looked visibly shaken.

'I heard you' she said. 'I know what you did.' She wiped at her eyes. 'You're not well, Leila' she said. 'And I will not let you get the better of me. More importantly, I will not allow this illness to take you over. It's a good job your next doctor's appointment is coming up. There are going to be big changes around here from now on.'

She went off downstairs leaving me feeling terrible. I went into a panic – what did she mean about interfering with my routine? I started to freak out. The more I thought about it the more anxious I got. My throat was tight and I started shaking. It was hard to breath. I forced myself to take deep breaths and slowly started to feel a bit better. I needed reassurance. I took my laptop off my desk and logged onto 'PerfectlyThin.' If none of my friends were online I would be in trouble. That thought set my anxiety off again and I was overcome with relief when I saw that Kate was in the chat room. I wasted no time.

Leila: Kate I'm scared. I had a row with Mum and I couldn't breathe

Kate: Calm down. It's a panic attack. Breathe slowly. What did you row about?

Leila: The usual. She caught me chucking up. She said she's going to make changes. I can't eat any more than I do Kate I can't

Kate: Calm down. Let's talk about something else. Do you want to see a photo of me?

Leila: Yes

Kate: Ok. I'm sending it now

Leila: Wow. OMG. You're pretty. Why are you wearing a nightdress?

Kate: I was in hospital

Leila: When?

Kate: Last year. They made me eat and I put on loads of weight. I did as I was told just to get out of there. I lost it all within 6 weeks. You see. They can't control us

Leila: You're right. Mum can't make me do anything. Thanks Kate

Kate: So when do I get a picture of you?

Leila: When I'm thin enough

Kate: That's never then…

Leila: LOL

I logged off the computer feeling slightly calmer, but still shaken after the row with Mum. It was getting dark outside and I went over the window to draw the curtains. I thought back to when I was little; these same curtains had given me nightmares. The pattern of large leaves had come alive at night time, twisting into menacing shapes. Without warning, The Voice started up.

You're not trying hard enough

I'm doing the best I can

You're eating way too much. You're kidding yourself if you think you'll ever be like those PerfectlyThin girls. You lack discipline

Maybe it was right, but there was so much opposition to me. It made me wonder sometimes if there was a grain of truth in what others were saying. Maybe I was thin.

Don't you dare try and oppose me. If you keep eating meals you will get fatter and fatter. Think what your stomach will be like then! It's big enough now

I wanted to scream. I put my hands over my ears to try and stop The Voice. As I turned to go back to my desk, a movement on the curtains caught my eye. The leaves swam together and expanded into a large black shadow which covered the wall. I turned round frantically, then looked back again. It was still there. It was much bigger than last time and I could clearly see a torso with arms and legs. It was coming towards me, arms outstretched. I screamed and closed my eyes. When I dared to open them again it was gone. I blinked hard. No, it was definitely no longer there. My head throbbed and I felt sick. I lay down on the bed. What if it had touched me? Was it real or could it be a ghost? I wanted to run into my mother's arms for comfort but she was too angry with me. Maybe I should just give in to The Voice, let it put its arms around me instead and go wherever it wanted to take me.

18

JENNA

I was on my way to school, walking slowly, trying to put my thoughts in order. I still hadn't got over what Mum and Dad had told me last night. I'd come down to get a hot chocolate before I went to bed. Mum and Dad were watching TV on the sofa. They both looked subdued.

'Has something happened?' I asked. I'd thought I had heard raised voices earlier when I was round at Charlie's; the walls are a bit thin between these houses.

'Sit down Jenna' Dad said, 'We want to have a chat with you.' I sat down anxiously on the end of the sofa. I knew it was about Leila. What had she done now?

Dad continued, 'Mum has found out tonight that Leila hasn't been eating as much as we thought. It's not really a surprise, we've probably been extremely naïve, but we wanted to be able to trust her.'

'She has been eating at school' I said, 'I see her every day in the canteen. The supervisor often sits with her; it takes up the whole lunch hour sometimes as she eats so slowly.'

'The woman must have the patience of a saint' said Mum

bitterly. 'This isn't very pleasant Jenna, but Leila has been making herself sick after her meals. At home, for sure and I wouldn't be surprised if it wasn't happening at school as well. I followed her upstairs tonight as I've had my suspicions for a while. That's what the row was about. School are doing their best, but I can't expect them to follow her around all day in such a big school. I'm going to insist that the Doctor takes this further. It's gone beyond our control and I don't like the effect it's having on everyone else. I'm going to have more say over what she eats at home. It's the only way I can be sure she's eating and keeping it down.'

'I hope the doctor can do something Mum' I said. 'I keep wondering what will happen if she doesn't stop.'

'That's not going to happen' said Dad firmly. He took Mum's hand in his. 'I'm going to take the day off tomorrow and come with you to the surgery. We need to regain the upper hand; otherwise she'll have to get treatment outside the home. But it won't come to that; between the three of us I'm sure we can make her see sense. I'll go up and have a word with her, let her know that we will both be going tomorrow.' He stood up, running his hand through his hair, making it stick out in all directions. He looked as drained as I felt. He trudged off upstairs. Mum switched the television on for the ten o clock news in a vain attempt to switch our attention to something else.

I hadn't slept very well, unsurprisingly. Then this morning, Leila had come running in from a walk in the park, announcing to us that from now on she was determined to get better. I didn't know what to believe. I set off for school, deep in thought. I was not in the mood for it but Mum wouldn't let me go to the doctor's with them. As I was crossing the road I heard someone calling out my name from across the street. I stopped and looked around. Damn. It was Kelsey, that strange girl from

Leila's class. It wasn't the first time she had approached me.

I waited as she crossed the road. Her black leather coat was flapping around her ankles.

'Hi Jenna' she said. 'Where's Leila?'

'She's not going to school today, she's got an appointment'

'What kind of appointment?' Kelsey asked.

'Leila can tell you when you see her' I said. Kelsey looked put out. Her long black hair trailed over her face but she made no effort to move it away.

'Lizzie said if she goes below five stone she'll die. Her mum said so. She needs to eat more.' Her eyes roved as she talked, her attention fixed somewhere in the distance.

'Don't say things like that. You don't know anything about it. Leila is fine.'

I turned away from her and ran off down the road, suddenly desperate to get to school. My legs were unsteady but I wanted to put as much distance between myself and Kelsey as possible.

19

LEILA

First thing on the morning of my doctor's appointment, I went off to the park for a cigarette. The sun was already up and despite its warm rays beating down on my face, I shivered, feeling chilly. I was always cold. While my friends were still going around in t-shirts and summer jackets, I needed to wear large woolly jumpers most of the time. Even huddling up to the radiator in my room didn't have much success at warming me up. I shoved my hands deep into my pockets, and walked faster.

The park was almost empty at this time of the morning, apart from the odd jogger and dog walker. As I neared the shelter, two middle aged women, clad in large t-shirts and running bottoms jogged past me, smiling. I attempted to smile back; it happened so little these days that I'd almost forgotten how to do it.

I lit my cigarette and took a deep drag, thinking back to last night, when Dad had come up to speak to me. I felt bad that he had taken a day off just to come to the doctor's with me.

I wanted to crawl into a little hole and hibernate. That way, everybody would have to leave me be.

It was turning into a lovely morning, but the cloud of depression was zapping the energy out of me. Every day was a battle. I didn't enjoy anything anymore. Mum looked really drawn and we could hardly be in the same room any more without arguing. Jenna kept out of my way most of the time, although I knew she was really keen on Charlie and spent a lot of time with him. As for my friends I hadn't been out with them since that horrible time in Café Blanco the other week. I had been round to Samia's a couple of times, but recently she'd started seeing this boy called George. He was a friend of her cousin. She'd fancied him for ages, ever since she met him at her cousin's birthday party last year. At school I got the impression that everyone was treading on eggshells around me, in case I kicked off. When I first had to go to the canteen, Samia and Cherry would offer to come with me, but I was adamant that they leave me alone. Too adamant I suppose. I was also annoyed with Kate. We'd been getting on so well that I'd suggested meeting up as she lived nearby, but every time I mentioned it she didn't give me an answer, as if she didn't want to see me. Maybe I was wrong to trust anyone, people always let me down. I might ask RosieB about it if I could get her on her own in the chat room, I'd looked at her profile and she was older than the rest of us and had been around a lot longer. She might be able to advise me what to do.

I shifted my weight. The cold stone bench was really uncomfortable on the bones of my buttocks and spine. At moments like this, I did register that I had lost a lot of weight. How could I hang onto that thought? The trouble was, whenever I looked in a mirror I could only see how enormous I was and The

Voice was rarely left me alone these days. The idea of putting on weight absolutely terrified me. There was no way I could walk down the street looking like I used to.

I thought back to when The Voice had compelled me to pull those awful faces all the time. I had fought against that and I had won. It had taken a tremendous amount of willpower, but if I had managed it once then I could do it again. I had been so close to banishing The Voice, but it had changed tactics and had caught me unawares. I knew I would have to dispel it again. Now that I could actually see The Voice when it spoke to me, maybe it was possible to get rid of it? It occurred to me that The Voice always caught me off my guard. What if I took charge?

I stood up, placing my feet firmly on the ground and looked up at the sky.

'Come on then Voice' I shouted. 'Show yourself now.' The wind whistled around me, but there was no buzzing noise. 'I'm not listening to your rubbish any more. Do you hear me Voice? I'm going to get better and you can't stop me.' Still no response but I felt stronger. I had to get back home quickly and tell Mum and Dad that I wanted them to see the doctor with me, so that we could fight this thing together. I jumped up and ran back across the park, hoping to get back before The Voice realised and caught up with me.

Sitting in the doctor's waiting room two hours later, I was scared again. I kept looking over my shoulder, terrified that The Voice would sneak up on me unawares. Finally, the nurse came out and called me into her room. I knew she was going to weigh me before my appointment. I had to strip to my underwear and turn my back to the scales so that I couldn't see the result. That was easier in a way, although I was convinced my weight would be pretty much the same as last time. When I was dressed again, she escorted me down to the doctor's room, where Mum and Dad were already seated, waiting for me. The nurse handed the doctor a piece of paper and shut the door behind her.

Dr Salmon consulted his notes. Mum told him about the new regime at school and how I was managing at home. I cringed as I knew that most of what she thought I was eating was not staying in my system. Dr Salmon turned to me.

'So young lady, how have you been finding it? Have you been eating lunch at school every day?' he boomed, loose strands of hair quivering on his head as he moved. I nodded.

'And what about the evening?' he asked. 'Do you eat a meal with your family?

I shook my head, 'I usually get it myself' I said, my voice sounding really small.

He laced his fingers together and looked over the top of his glasses at me.

'I gave you the benefit of the doubt last time' he said, 'And gave you a chance to prove to everyone that you did not have a problem eating, which is what you led me to believe.' He looked at Mum. 'The situation has changed now. Leila has lost over a stone since I last saw her, which means she is significantly underweight.' Mum gasped and my brain whirred around, trying to work out what the scales had read. Despite my good intentions, I still couldn't help being relieved that I hadn't put any weight on. Dr Salmon continued.

'You obviously haven't been eating enough and your mother tells me you are still exercising and she suspects you have vomited up food on occasion.' I wanted the ground to swallow me up and fixed my eyes firmly on the floor. He continued, addressing Mum and Dad.

'I am going to refer Leila to the Eating Disorders unit at the hospital as an Outpatient, but the appointment may take a couple of weeks to come through. She will have to try not to lose any more weight; otherwise she will need to be admitted as an inpatient. I hope she can avoid that by eating more at home. Exercise needs to stop. Look at me Leila' he said.

I reluctantly looked up at his face. I didn't find it so funny now.

'Listen to me carefully' he said. 'Your parents will help you' he said, 'But you will have to let your mother take control of the food you eat at home. She is trying to help you, you must understand that. She is not your enemy. If you cooperate with her, then you may be able to continue your treatment at home. If, however, you persist in losing weight, you will be admitted to hospital. I know it's going to be difficult for you, so I am also going to make you an appointment to see our counsellor here at the practice. She's a very nice lady. You can talk things through with her. Luckily she has some experience in this area. I think she will help you if you can bring yourself to trust her.' He stood up.

'Wait here a moment, I'll just go and speak to the receptionist about setting up this referral. It will give you a minute to talk.'

He left the room and shut the door gently. I suddenly felt completely overwhelmed and burst into tears. I turned to Mum who was sitting next to me and fell into her arms. She stroked my hair and dabbed at her eyes.

'I'm sorry Mum,' I said, 'and Dad.' I took a deep breath. 'I still mean what I said to you earlier this morning. I'm going to try really hard to beat this and I'll try to let you help me.'

Dad spoke for the first time since we had got there. 'I hope you do mean it Leila, because this is serious now. You can see that can't you?' I nodded. At that moment the Doctor came back in.

'I've made you an appointment with the counsellor.' He handed Mum an appointment card. 'You should be hearing from the hospital within the next two weeks. If Leila loses any more weight, I need you to let me know and we will have to speed things up. However, I'm hoping we've caught this early enough, before her behaviour becomes too entrenched.'

'Come on then' said Dad. He held out his hand to Dr Salmon. 'Thank you' he said, and we all trooped forlornly out of the office. Anxiously I hoped I would be able to live up to my side of the bargain.

The Voice

The Voice was temporarily thrown. The girl's mind was growing in strength again. How dare she? The Voice decided to retreat for a while, regain some momentum. Then it would return – with a vengeance.

20

LEILA

I had kept my promise. I'd eaten a meal with the family. I'd hated every minute of it but I was determined. It was after the meal that the worst part started, when I had to try not to think. It was agony. I was sitting on the sofa with Jenna when the battle started. A buzzing began in my right ear. I knew it would be back.

'Let's watch Eastenders' I said to Jenna, deliberately ignoring it.

She picked up the remote and switched channels. The familiar tune started up, drowning the buzzing slightly.

'Tell me what's been happening' I urged Jenna and tried to give her my full attention.

What do you think you are doing?

I jumped. Jenna gave me a look and squeezed my arm.

'Keep talking' I said.

Look at lazy Leila sitting on the sofa – no wonder you're fat! Isn't it time you did some exercise?

I fixed my eyes on the television screen. It was pointless.

Why aren't you burning off calories do you want to get fat?

'Shut up!' I whispered
Lily looked up at me from the floor, where she was doing a jigsaw. 'The telly can't hear you, silly.'

You think you can ignore me don't you?

I fixed my eyes on the TV screen.

Really? Let's see.

A roaring filled my ears and to my horror a shape loomed up behind the TV. It was dark, yet transparent. This time there was no doubt, it was a person. I looked at my sisters – why couldn't they see it? The figure was huge. It flickered in and out of sight, making my eyes hurt and my head spin. I closed my eyes and screamed 'Get it away from me.'
Lily jumped to her feet. 'Turn the TV off Jenna! Leila doesn't like it.'
'Go and get Mum Lily' said Jenna. Lily scampered out of the door.
'What is it?' Jenna's voice in my ear was soft and soothing in comparison to the rasping harshness of The Voice.
I burst into tears.
'Leila, it's only Eastenders.' She looked at me and I started laughing. I was hysterical but I couldn't stop.
Mum came in, wiping her hands on a dishcloth. 'Your father never washes up properly' she said, 'I always have to redo it. What's going on here?'

I wiped my face. 'Nothing' I said. 'Can I go upstairs now Mum?' I asked. I knew what I had to do.

I went upstairs to the bathroom and ran myself a really hot bath. Clouds of steam blurred my vision. I undressed and stared at my fat thighs, then pounded them angrily with my fists. I could be made to eat but I couldn't be made to like the way I looked. While the water was running, I took out the razor blade that I'd managed to remove from a disposable razor and cut angrily across my thighs. The blood beaded onto the surface, then flowed in a rush. I wished I were cutting into the vocal cords of The Voice, destroying it in one fell swoop. Pain rocketed through me, but that I could deal with far easier than I could handle The Voice. I closed my eyes and let the waves of pain wash over me. I relaxed back against the wall, relieved to feel some tension fading away. The painful stinging soothed me. I wrapped some strips of an old sheet around my legs. I sat with a towel over my legs, waiting for the bleeding to stop. I had made a real breakthrough today with my food, nobody could deny me that. This was different anyhow; it was completely separate from my problems with eating. This was one secret I was not going to share. Not even on PerfectlyThin.

21

JENNA

I was walking back from seeing a hilarious romcom at the cinema with Charlie. My English teacher had recommended we all see a new version of an old Shakespeare drama that had just come out but I didn't tell Charlie that. I didn't understand a word of the play when we read it in class and I didn't want him to think I was stupid, so had suggested a comedy instead. The cinema was pretty full as the film had just come out. We'd bought an enormous carton of popcorn, which would have disgusted Mum as she is always going on about how popcorn should be banned from cinemas on account of smell, noise, mess et cetera, and I felt really content. The film was very funny and I laughed more than I had done for ages. It was definitely the right choice; Shakespeare would probably have had me in tears – and not from laughter.

We'd taken the scenic route home along the canal. I loved walking by the water, even if it was murky and green in places.

'It's Mum I feel sorry for' I was telling Charlie. 'She usually gets dinner ready for about six o' clock, so Leila comes down at least an hour before and hangs around fussing over everything she does, watching her like a hawk. She goes mad if it's not ready at six on the dot. If I were Mum I would have lost it by now. It's such an obsession; I hadn't realised how bad it was. Can you imagine?'

'Yes I can actually. Molly was the same. She practically took over the kitchen, started baking cakes all the time. Never ate them of course – mind you I quite enjoyed that phase!'

'Greedy pig!' I nudged him and he laughed. I put my arm through his and slid my hand into his jacket pocket.

'Is your hand cold?' he asked. I nodded. I couldn't believe it when he took my hand out of his pocket and held it in his. 'That's better' he said. 'I've wanted to do that for ages.' He smiled at me, checking that it was ok and I beamed back at him, trying to look cool. My heart was beating so fast I was convinced he must be able to hear it. Was this really happening to me? I hoped my palms wouldn't get sweaty. Luckily there were hardly any other people around and I had the moment for myself. We walked in contented silence most of the way home.

I came back down to earth with a bang as I turned my key in the front door lock and became aware of shouting from inside. I groaned. Leila and Mum were going at each other hammer and tongs in the kitchen. I was tempted to go back out and avoid the situation; instead I took a deep breath before going in to join them. Leila was sat at the kitchen table sobbing and Mum was standing at the sink wringing the dish cloth out furiously in her hands.

'What's going on?' I asked nervously. Mum and Leila both started to answer at once, but Mum's voice was louder.

'Leila doesn't like what I'm cooking for dinner tonight.

It's just food, Leila and you need to eat more of it, not fuss about what goes into it. I still don't think you're eating enough to maintain your weight.'

Leila snapped back 'I can't believe you Mum. You know I've been making such an effort and I'm eating so much more than I used to. How can you try and force me to eat more? If you're going to do that then I won't eat anything ever again' she said and rushed off upstairs. Mum sat down and put her head in her hands.

'I might have known it was all going too smoothly', she said, 'but she doesn't eat enough to keep her weight up, even though I can see she is trying. The doctor said we had to let him know if she was losing any more weight, but she won't let me anywhere near the scales. I've been biting my tongue, trying so hard not to say anything, but I lost my rag this afternoon. Now I've probably set her right back again.'

I didn't know what to say. It was like living in a war zone and I wanted it to stop.

I went upstairs to talk to Leila but she was having a bath and obviously didn't want to talk to me. A bit later I heard her leave the house, shouting out 'I'm going out' as she slammed the door behind her. That meant she'd miss dinner but Mum didn't bother to try and stop her. She left me looking after Lily and went off round to Helen's with a bottle of wine. No sooner had she gone than Charlie turned up. Despite the drama around me my heart still jumped up and down when he came into the room.

'Your mum has just come over looking very determined' he said, 'so I thought I'd leave them to it.' I told him what had been going on, then Lily came down insisting we give her a game of Junior Scrabble. It was fun and we let Lily win, so she went off up to bed happy. Charlie and I snuggled up on the sofa and were like that when Mum came home. She did a bit of a double take when she saw us and Charlie quickly disentangled himself from me, but then she smiled and went into the kitchen to make some tea. How could she not like Charlie?

Charlie made his exit soon after and Mum came and sat next to me on the sofa. 'Jenna' she said, 'I'm really pleased that you and Charlie are getting on so well, but I am a little concerned about your age. Don't you think you are a bit young to have a boyfriend?'

'Mum' I protested, cringing. I did not want to have this conversation, but it looked like I didn't have much choice. 'Charlie and I are good friends, that's all, you needn't worry. You know how sensible I am.' I tried to make a joke out of it.

Mum didn't look convinced and I must admit for the first time I doubted myself. I was sensible – usually, but lately my feelings were getting harder to control, and somehow, I didn't really care so much about doing the right thing these days.

22

LEILA

I slammed the door behind me as hard as I could. I was annoyed with Mum, but also with myself. I was too weak to do battle with The Voice. I was escaping to Samia's. I hadn't been to her house for a bit and no way was I eating tonight.

'Leila' Samia pulled me into a big hug. 'Come upstairs, I'm so glad you came.'

She dragged me up the narrow staircase and I collapsed onto the bed. My energy levels were low today. 'Have you been ok?' she asked. 'You haven't been coming round as much lately.'

'I know,' I replied. 'I've been doing a lot of my coursework. Besides, haven't you got a boyfriend now?'

Samia blushed, but her face lit up. 'He's great, Leila. We have so much in common. He's in a band called 'The Underdogs' and they're really good. He's going to be playing some gigs soon - you'll have to come along.'

I nodded although the idea didn't particularly thrill me. Going out was a bit stressful these days as there were so many things to worry about.

'I can't wait for you to meet him' she said. She suddenly sat up, excited. 'Hey, I've had a great idea. I'm meeting him later. Why don't you come along?'

I was disappointed. I'd wanted Samia all to myself this evening. The last thing I wanted was to meet her boyfriend. It was one thing Samia dating but even my little sister seemed to be getting ahead of me. She had been getting really close to Charlie and I could see she liked him a lot. It made me feel inadequate. I'd never been particularly interested in boys. When I did come across boys in social situations I felt terribly awkward. One time I had been to a teenage disco organised for charity at school. When the slow dance came on at the end and boys started shuffling across to the girls on the opposite side of the hall I scooted off to hide in the toilet. Who would want to go out with me? Besides, now that I was so horrified by the way I looked, there was no way I wanted anybody getting up close and personal with me. But Samia was looking eagerly at me and I didn't want to disappoint her. 'Ok' I said.

'Great' she said. 'We're meeting in McDonald's at seven o'clock.'

My heart sank. I couldn't go to McDonald's. My reluctance must have expressed itself on my face, because Samia's smile disappeared as quickly as it had appeared.

'What's the matter?' she said. 'You don't have to eat anything.' She went quiet after that and started chewing her finger. Suddenly she stood up.

'I can't deal with this, Leila. It's too upsetting for me. Look at you! You're half the size you used to be and you can't see it can you? I want to be your friend but you never want to do anything with us. If it involves food then you look terrified but we can't just go to the park all the time. It's getting colder now and you're always frozen so it can't be much fun for you. I want to do normal stuff with you, like we used to.' She sat down again on the bed, looking upset. 'You look so miserable, Lee, I can't bear it. I'm really happy about George and I'd love you to meet him, but he won't see the happy, funny friend that I used to hang around with. I hate your diet; I hate what this is doing to you. You aren't you anymore.'

I couldn't say anything in my defence. She was right. I didn't enjoy anything much these days. I wanted to be on my own most of the time, in situations that I could control. McDonald's was scary not just because of the food, but loads of girls from school hung out there and I was scared of them making snide comments, like they sometimes did at school. Jenna had told me Lizzie had said I might die if I didn't start eating more! What kind of nonsense was that? I didn't want to put myself in the firing line if it was in any way avoidable.

'I'm sorry' was all I could manage. 'I'll meet George another time.' I grabbed my bag. 'I have to go now.'

I stumbled to my feet and quickly ran down the stairs and out of the house before she could react. I was embarrassed and was wishing that I'd never come in the first place. Samia's house was yet another safe place that I would have to strike off my list. My world was getting increasingly smaller. As I slammed a door behind me for the second time that evening, I felt the depression cloud weighing heavily on my shoulders. Determined not to succumb, I forced myself into a jog. I would not let my mood slow me down. I had let myself go lately, falling for peoples lies about my need to put on weight. I had let people get the better of me and I had temporarily lost sight of the fact that I still had half a stone to lose. I picked up my pace as I headed towards home. I wouldn't let myself be tricked this time.

I stopped in the alleyway by our house for a few minutes before I let myself in as I didn't want anyone to see that I had been running. I didn't care what they thought but if I could avoid an argument then it was worth the subterfuge. The house was quiet when I went in. The television wasn't on which was unusual in our house. I stuck my head round the living room door and I was surprised to see Dad sat on the sofa, with his headphones on. He took them off and motioned to me to come over. I hadn't seen much of Dad lately and for once I didn't feel like going upstairs and being by myself. I snuggled up next to him on the sofa.

'Where have you been?' he asked.

'To Samia's' I said.

'Was it fun?' he asked.

'Not really' I said. I didn't want to lie to him. 'I had a row with Mum and then Samia sort of had a go at me so I came home.'

'Did you have dinner?' he asked

'No' I said, for once I couldn't be bothered to lie.

'You're not getting better Leila are you?' he asked. I shook my head.

'I meant what I said at the doctor's, but it's taken me over again.' The Voice had started buzzing in my ears again and I was unable to resist.

He sighed. 'I can see how hard it is for you' he said. 'Mum loses her temper I know, but she doesn't mean to. Unfortunately I realise that until you want to beat this thing there is nothing any of us can do about it. And I don't think you do want to get better yet do you? Be honest?' he said.

'Sometimes I do, but mostly I don't' I admitted.

Dad gave me a hug. 'You'll break my heart, Leila' he said, 'If you don't get well. So you'd better start trying sometime soon, before it's too late.'

I felt as if my heart had been ripped out, but then The Voice started whispering seductively and what it said made complete sense.

'I'll try Dad' I said, hating myself for lying. Maybe it was best for everybody if I did die. I was causing far too much grief around me. I wondered whether I could run away. Then I wouldn't have to eat and I would soon be forgotten and no longer cause any worry. At that moment there was a squeal and Lily burst into the room. 'Leila' she yelled and threw herself into my lap. I winced at the weight of her but tried not to show it. 'Will you read me a bedtime story?' she asked, her big blue eyes fixing on mine. 'You haven't done one for ages and you do the best voices' she pleaded.

'Come on' I said, taking her hand, realising how stupid I was being. I couldn't turn my back on Lily, or Dad, or Mum, or Jenna. They would hurt terribly if I were to disappear. 'I'll do my best voices' I said, praying that I could find one strong enough voice to silence the other Voice, the one that was tearing everything around me to pieces.

The Voice

The Voice was muttering. It was time to take drastic action. No more pussy footing around. It was time for Phase Three. No mind could resist such pressure. The Voice took a deep breath, and let out an almighty roar.

23

JENNA

Leila woke me up early. 'Be quiet' I mumbled as she tapped her way around the room. At last the door closed. I opened one eye and jabbed my finger at my mobile – Six am – Leila was definitely getting worse. Even on a school day I never set my alarm before seven fifteen. No doubt she'd be downstairs now, pretending to have breakfast. I was sick of it.

I shut my eyes and dozed a little. I'd never been a morning person and I probably would have been asleep for the next hour if I hadn't been awoken by shouting from downstairs. Mum and Leila, of course. Dad left very early for work most mornings – and I suspected he was getting out of the house as soon as he could to avoid the constant arguments over meal times. I hated the way the day was starting and I turned over onto my stomach and yelled into my pillow. I was so fed up with my family. Lately I had found myself staying on at after school clubs, just to avoid coming home, as I never knew what kind of battle zone I would be entering into. The tension was unbearable. Lying in bed, thinking about everything, I suddenly realised what a large part of the problem was. A lump formed in my throat. I missed my sister.

I was roused from my thoughts by a grating noise as the bedroom door slid open and Lily shuffled in. She was wearing her school uniform which looked incredibly cute. Her hair was loose over her shoulders and she was holding a hairbrush in her hand.

'Hi Lily,' I said. 'What's up?'

It was very unusual for her to come into my bedroom so early in the morning.

'Mummy hasn't done my hair yet' she said. 'Can you do it for me?'

I swung my legs out of bed and Lily clambered up and sat on the edge of the bed. She was looking forlorn.

'Jenna' she said. 'Why do Mummy and Leila argue all the time? They're shouting downstairs and I'm supposed to be going to school. What's wrong with Leila?'

I sighed inside. How was I supposed to explain to Lily what was going on? I wasn't sure how much Mum wanted her to know. I decided on the easy option.

'Leila's a teenager, Lily. Teenagers are moody and horrible and argue with their parents – it's part of growing up. I'll be turning horrible next' I joked, but Lily looked alarmed. 'I'm only messing. Come here. Let's forget all about them and their silly arguments. How about we do something nice together after school? Would you like to come with me to Charlie's and we can play with baby Olivia?' Lily beamed and nodded vigorously. I took her into my arms and we had a big hug together. I would have to get Mum to say something to her as I didn't want to have to shoulder the responsibility. It was bad enough looking out for

Leila all the time. It would be nice if someone could look after me for a change.

I sat Lily up and finished plaiting her hair. I could no longer hear voices downstairs. The front door slammed, then Mum yelled up the stairs.

'Jenna, are you ready for school yet?'

Lily ran over to the door and shouted to Mum as she ran downstairs. 'Jenna's done my hair Mummy and she's taking me to see baby Olivia after school.'

I scrambled out of bed and hurried into the bathroom. I splashed my face and spent a lot less time brushing my hair than I had Lily's, then rushed downstairs.

'You're going to be late, Jenna. You need to leave more time for your breakfast.'

'Stop worrying Mum, a piece of toast will do.' I grabbed a slice from the plate that was lying on the table. I didn't tell Mum I had nearly been late every day this week. She had enough to worry about. I gave her a quick kiss.

'See you later Mum. Don't forget I'm taking Lily next door after school.'

'There's no danger of that – Lily won't let me forget.'

I grabbed my bag and ran off down the road. With a bit of luck, I would just about make it to registration in time.

24

LEILA

The Voice dragged me out of a deep sleep. The streetlight cast a dim glow over the room. The shadow was back on the wall. This time it was enormous. It was female, breasts and hips clearly visible despite the rolls of fat layered around the torso. Two burning red eyes stared at me. I couldn't move. The shadow threw back its head and laughed, a cold sound that chilled my body. As the laugh got louder, the shape wobbled from side to side, mocking me. For once, The Voice was silent, but I didn't need to hear it to get the message. I ran my hands over my hip-bones, terrified that layers of fat had covered them in the night. They jutted sharply and I caressed them lovingly, relief washing over me. The Voice needed no words to remind me.

I didn't sleep after that and got up at six. I was so tired I didn't hear Mum coming into the kitchen and she caught me breaking up a slice of toast and throwing it into the bin. She went mental. I was too tired to argue and walked out in the middle of her rant.

'It's a good job your hospital appointment has come

through' she shouted after me, 'You won't be able to carry on like this for much longer.'

'Stuff the hospital' I yelled as I ran down the path, crashing into Charlie as he went past on his way to school. 'Watch where you're going' I shouted at him. I lit a cigarette as I stomped off down the High Street on my way to school, not caring that I was in uniform and would be in serious trouble if a teacher spotted me.

I inhaled deeply and blew out a cloud of smoke. What was up with Kate last night? I could remember our conversation word for word as I had been over it looking for clues.

Leila: Hi Kate

Kate: Hi Leila

Leila: I've missed you

Kate: Mum wouldn't let me go online. She took my computer away. I'm at my aunt's house

Leila: I thought you were avoiding me

Kate: Idiot!

Leila: Tell me about it. I've got hospital next week I'm scared and I have to see a counsellor

Kate: Counsellors are easy. Tell them what they want to hear

Leila: Really?

Kate: Trust me

Leila: What about you?

Kate: I lost more weight. Mum is going mad. She won't let me out of her sight. Except for this evening she had to work that's why I'm at my aunt's but she's easy to get round

Leila: Is that why we can't meet up?

Kate: Stop asking me that. I'm too fat to see anyone

Leila: You're not fat in the photo, you're lovely
Kate: That was last year.
Leila: How much do you weigh now?
Kate: I don't know
Leila: I bet you're tiny
Kate: Whatever. Stop going on about it! I hate myself

She had suddenly logged off. What did that mean? Had her aunt come into the room or was she in a bad way? Was she cross with me? I was jealous of her in that photo. I wanted to be the thinnest.

At lunchtime I didn't even go to the canteen. I'd excused myself from lesson to go to the toilet but instead of signing for a toilet pass had gone straight up to the old toilet block at the top of the building. Not many people could be bothered to go up there, not even the smokers, who had a much better spot behind the bushes at the back of the school playground. The compulsion was overwhelmingly strong today. It was not a question of whether to give into it, but when. The idea that had started as a tiny fluttering at the back of my mind was now drowning out any other thoughts. By the end of the morning I could no longer ignore it. There was only one way to silence it.

I didn't normally do this at school but today I had no choice. I opened my school bag and checked that it was still there. If they'd found it at school I would be kissing goodbye to Stenfield Academy. A girl in Year eight had been chucked out straight away for having a penknife on her. That was a firm rule in school and there were no exceptions, whatever the reason for carrying it. Smoking paled in comparison to this crime, but my intentions were honourable; my only war was with myself.

The corridors were quiet that lunchtime, particularly as a staff against students rounders tournament was taking place on the playing field. I could hear girls jeering and whistling outside already. Any opportunity to see the teachers making fools of themselves was a big crowd puller. I went into the girl's toilets and quickly checked the three cubicles to make sure there was no one there. I locked myself into the furthest one, then sat down on the closed seat and quickly extracted the razor blade. I unfolded Dad's large white handkerchief which I'd stashed it in and pulled my skirt up over my right thigh. I gave myself no time to hesitate, drawing the blade and slicing it across the fat of my thigh. God, I hated my legs more than I hated my head. As the ruby red drops emerged onto my leg, I closed my eyes and let out a deep sigh. The relief was instantaneous. I quickly seized the handkerchief and tied it hard around my leg, preparing to start on the next one.

I was just smoothing down my skirt when I heard the outside door being wrenched open and heavy footsteps approaching.

'Who's in there?' demanded a voice. The voice was quiet, but to me sounded menacing.

Oh no. Kelsey. What was she doing here? She must have followed me.

I had managed to avoid Kelsey since the episode in Café Blanco, but she still seemed to be very interested in knowing my business. Since it had become obvious to my classmates that I'd been having problems, Kelsey had not stopped trying to pump me – or even Jenna – for information. I didn't trust her one inch. I feared Kelsey could be a bit unstable after I'd witnessed the fight that she'd had with Julia that time. I knew Cherry thought

I was a bit paranoid about her as she came across as being very reserved, but that was what unnerved me; her quiet persistence and dogged determination to find out what I was up to.

'I know you're in there, Leila,' she called, poking her foot under the cubicle door.

I grabbed the blade which was wrapped up in the handkerchief and shoved it into the top of my bag and smoothed my skirt carefully down over my leg. My hands were trembling. Reluctantly I opened the cubicle door and stepped out to face Kelsey. She was staring at the mirror and our eyes met in the glass.

Kelsey turned to face me. 'Are you ok? You left History early. Why aren't you out watching the game?'

'I just needed the loo. What's it to you anyway?' Why didn't she go away? My leg was smarting and I needed to sort myself out properly. The interruption to my ritual made me feel very nervous as I hadn't finished off in the proper way. Kelsey stared at me again and I cast my eyes down to avoid her gaze. My anxiety grew as I had lost track of time and had no idea whether the lesson bell was about to go off at any moment.

As I looked down I noticed with horror that a line of blood had started to seep through my skirt. I couldn't help letting out a gasp before I could stop myself. Kelsey looked down too and let out a shriek.

'Leila haven't you got a tampon?' she shrieked. 'Here, give us your bag while you sort your skirt out.'

Kelsey reached out to take my bag and I made a grab for the handkerchief before Kelsey could get it and held onto my bag with my left hand. No way was I letting her see the blade.

'Leave me alone' I shouted.

Kelsey yanked the bag away from me. 'I'm trying to help you, what's the matter with you?' she yelled. 'OMG look at your leg. Let me see.' With no warning, she lunged forward at me.

Kelsey was twice the size of me and I was so focused on not letting her get the handkerchief that I couldn't manage to keep hold of the bag. Kelsey yanked the bag close to her chest, a knowing expression spreading across her face. She was looking me up and down and started slowly nodding her head.

'I bet you don't get periods do you? Anorexics don't, everyone knows that. So what's the matter with your leg? Let me see.'

'Please leave me alone' I gasped. Tears started pouring down my face. This couldn't be happening. Not now, not like this. I squeezed the handkerchief tightly and winced as the blade dug into my hand. I was desperate that she shouldn't see the blade but had forgotten how sharp it was. Kelsey didn't miss a trick, her eyes narrowing as I cried out in pain.

'What have you got in your hand?' she cried. She lunged forward and tried to grab the handkerchief. I reacted instinctively, trying to hold on to it and keep it away from her, but there was a ping as the razor blade clattered out from the handkerchief onto the floor. Frantically, I bent down to pick it up but Kelsey leant over me and her weight knocked me to the floor.

'I'm trying to help you' she shouted.

I threw myself up against her and felt a searing pain in my arm. I looked down. Blood was pouring out of a gash in my lower arm. The pain was intense and waves of nausea and light-headedness rippled up and down my body. I fell back onto the floor aware that Kelsey had started to make a really strange gasping sound and her face was racked with anxiety as she stared down at me, rooted to the spot. All of a sudden she ripped off her tie and bent down to wind it round my arm, attempting to stop the bleeding. She pressed down on my arm with her right hand and rooted around frantically in her bag with her other hand, pulling out her mobile phone. She pressed a button and the last thing I remember is her gasping 'ambulance, quick' before everything went blissfully black.

25

JENNA

I first had an inkling that something was up at the beginning of the first lesson of the afternoon. It was double English and we were getting our books out to carry on with reading 'Romeo and Juliet' together in class. 'Please don't pick me' I prayed silently. I sat in the far corner hoping to be out of Miss Gregory's sightline.

Miss Gregory had just selected Melody Dyer to read – Melody loves reading and is really good at it. It would save a lot of messing around and anguish if she just let her read for the whole lesson, but that would be too easy. Before Melody could even open her mouth the door opened and Mrs Paris came in, looking serious. She had a quick word with Miss Gregory then addressed the class.

'Girls there has been an incident in school and for Health and Safety reasons, we need to evacuate this corridor.' An excited gasp went up in the room and everybody started talking at once. She held up her hand for silence. 'I need you to be sensible as we need to move as quickly and QUIETLY as possible. There is nothing to worry about, you aren't in any danger' she added. 'You are to all gather up your things and follow Miss Gregory downstairs. You will continue the lesson in the hall.' Mary raised her eyebrows at me as she picked our bags up off the floor and I was just about to whisper to her when I heard Mrs Paris say 'Jenna Summers, will you wait behind please. The rest of you follow me.'

There was a flurry of activity as the class picked up their bags and coats and followed Mrs Paris. Mary squeezed my arm and gave me an anxious glance as she followed the others outside. I was feeling extremely bewildered; what was going on? Once everyone was out in the corridor, Mrs Paris came back in and shut the door behind her.

'You need to come with me Jenna. I'm afraid there's been a very serious incident and your sister Leila was involved.'

'Leila?' I gasped, 'Is she ok?'

'Leila has been hurt and is on her way to hospital now. She's in the best possible place' Mrs Paris reassured me, 'I'm sorry I can't tell you more at the moment, but your mother is on her way over, which is why I want you to stay in school.'

'Was she in a fight?' I asked. I couldn't imagine Leila fighting; she was so frail she wouldn't be much of an opponent for anyone, despite her temper.

'I'm sorry I can't discuss it at the moment' she said, 'The police are here and will no doubt explain everything to your parents.' I must have gone a bit pale as Mrs Paris pulled out a chair and helped me to sit on it. 'I'm sorry love' she said, 'I know it's a real shock for you.'

She was right. I suddenly felt horribly sick. The police? What on earth had happened?

'Can we go and see if Mum is here?' I asked, and she nodded and led the way out and down the corridor.

The school felt deserted already. As it was warm and all the windows were open the noise of excited students being led down to the hall carried through the air. I shivered, despite the warmth. I was frightened. Mrs Paris took me to the waiting area outside the Head's room and went off to see if Mum had arrived. I rummaged around in the bottom of my bag and got my phone out. I wanted to send Charlie a text but at that moment I heard footsteps coming down the corridor and I dropped my phone back into my bag. Mrs Paris came in followed by Mum. I was so relieved to see her I flung my arms around her and burst into tears. 'What's happened Mum?' I asked, 'Where's Leila?'

Mrs Paris motioned us both to sit down. 'Mrs Summers, Leila and another student were involved in an incident at lunchtime in the toilet block upstairs. Leila is ok,' she stressed, 'but she appears to have been stabbed in the arm.'

Mum's hands flew to her open mouth.

'She lost a lot of blood and fainted at the scene so she has been taken to hospital by ambulance. The police will be accompanying Leila and a car will take you to the hospital. We have no idea what happened at the moment as the girls appear to have been on their own, but PC Ellis our on-site Police Officer is downstairs investigating what happened.'

Thoughts were whizzing around in my head. Leila fighting didn't make sense. Fights happened from time to time in school, but a stabbing? That kind of stuff only happened in the news. Mum looked as white as a ghost and was staring in disbelief at Mrs Paris.

'How seriously is Leila injured?' she asked. 'She is going to be alright, isn't she?' Her voice was much higher than usual.

'The paramedics had stabilised her before they put her in the ambulance' replied Mrs Paris. Her voice went down a notch as she added, 'I want you to know that I do recognise the seriousness of the situation and the school will do everything in its power to find out exactly what happened.'

There was a knock at the door and a uniformed police woman came in. I was relieved to see it was PC Ellis. I'd never had any dealings with her before but she had a really friendly smile and I found her presence around the school reassuring. 'Mrs Summers?' she asked. 'I've come to escort you to the hospital. Your husband is meeting us there and we will be able to tell you exactly what is going on. Try not to worry, Leila is in good hands.'

As we followed the police officer down to the car park, Mum took my hand in hers. We were both too shocked to speak. I wondered who the other student was and what on earth had happened? I'd been worrying recently about my sister going into hospital but under an entirely different set of circumstances. I desperately wanted to see that she was ok and get some answers. None of this made any sense at all.

26

LEILA

From black to white. I opened my eyes to a sea of whiteness. White walls, white ceiling, a fluorescent light and a lady in a white coat. I shut my eyes again. My arm felt heavy and sore and my throat was desperately dry. I suddenly remembered what had happened, opened my eyes and sat bolt upright. The white coated lady rushed over and eased me back down again. A nurse. I must be in hospital. My right arm was bandaged up and my left arm was hooked up to a drip. What were they putting in me? I tried to reach to pull out the drip but my arm wouldn't move. I was trapped. There was a movement at the door of the room and Mum came rushing in.

'Leila' she cried. 'You're awake. Oh thank goodness.' The nurse said something to Mum but she spoke so softly I couldn't catch what she had said.

'Mum, I said. What's in this drip? I don't want anything in me; please can you take it out?'

'Leila you're being rehydrated, that's all. You've had a nasty shock and lost a lot of blood. Try to relax. What on earth happened?'

I cast my mind back and a picture took shape in my mind of Kelsey tussling with me on the floor. With horror I remembered that I had been cutting my leg in school. I furtively eased up the sheet and looked down to see what I was wearing. Relieved, I realised I was still wearing the Lycra gym shorts I had taken to wearing under my clothes, so that nobody could see the scars on my legs. How was I going to explain what had happened? I was so frightened that Mum would find out that I started to cry. I would just have to pretend I couldn't remember until I worked out what to do.

'When can I come off this drip Mum?' I asked. The idea of having some unknown liquid going into my body was freaking me out big time. I knew it would be laced with sugar and I would balloon up if I was stuck in this bed for much longer. 'I feel much better now' I said. The pain in my arm was excruciating.

'Oh Leila' she said. 'Don't you realise how serious this is? You've been stabbed and you need to relax and recover. You're weak enough as it is without this. Your blood pressure is way too low. Let the nurses look after you and give you whatever you need.' She sounded exasperated.

I closed my eyes in frustration. I couldn't believe what was happening. To make matters worse it was my right hand. How would I do my school work? Already my concentration was dodgy; now my arm was messed up. If stupid Kelsey hadn't interfered none of this would have happened.

The door opened and PC Ellis from school came in. She smiled at me and sat down next to me on the bed. She patted my leg. 'I'm so glad to see you are awake now' she said. I wished I wasn't. It was like a bad dream. 'Are you ok to answer a few questions?' she said.

I was in turmoil. I couldn't think what to say.

'It's all a bit of a blur' I said. 'I'm too tired to think.'

'I understand it's hard for you' said PC Ellis, 'but we do need to know what happened as soon as possible. I've spoken to Kelsey already; she is maintaining that it was all an accident and she has no idea where the weapon came from.'

'That's ridiculous' said Mum. PC Ellis held up her hand, 'Let me hear what Leila has to say.' I realised I wasn't going to get out of this conversation, even if I did manage to stall her she would only be back the next day. It was bad enough being pinned down in that bed with who knows what substance slithering its poison into my body. I might as well get it over with.

'I left lesson early because I couldn't face going to lunch. I'm sorry Mum' I apologised. At least that would be nothing new for her to digest. 'Kelsey must have followed me up to that toilet; why else would she have been there? She has got a bit of a thing about me – ask Jenna. The whole point is that not many people go there, that's why I chose it.'

'Talk me through what happened' said PC Ellis.

'I was in the cubicle when Kelsey came in and called me' I said. 'She wanted me to go to lunch with her and I refused. I said I had my lunch in my bag and I wanted to eat it on my own. She didn't believe me so she was trying to grab my bag, to see whether it had food in it, I suppose.' I paused and mentally crossed my fingers. 'We got into a tussle as she was trying to pull my bag off me and she knocked me over. It was an accident,' I insisted, looking at PC Ellis for reassurance. 'The next thing I knew my arm was really stinging and there was blood everywhere. I don't know where the blade came from' I lied, 'but it was totally an accident.'

PC Ellis was nodding slowly. 'Good girl' she said 'You're

146

doing really well. I just need to clarify a few things. You say you don't know where the weapon came from?' I shook my head. 'Yet we have taken fingerprints from the blade and both yours and Kelsey's are on it.' How do you explain that?' she sat patiently, waiting for an answer.

'I must have touched it in the scuffle' I said. 'I don't remember.'

'The prints are good ones' she said, 'which would indicate that you had actually taken hold of the blade. Are you sure you didn't pick it up? How else would your hand get cut?'

I looked down at my bandaged hand. 'Maybe I did' I said 'It all happened so quickly.'

'OK' she said and stood up. 'That's enough for now. I'll have another chat with Kelsey and see if she can remember any more. As you know any student found with a weapon faces instant exclusion, so I do need to know how it got into school, but I don't want you to worry. You get some rest now and I'll be back to see you tomorrow.'

The nurse who had been hovering around in the background the whole time came over to my bedside. 'I think Leila needs to get some sleep now' she said. 'Is that alright Mum? You can come back tomorrow. She's in good hands here.'

Mum gave me a kiss and as much of a hug as she could, trying to avoid my arms. 'I want to come home Mum' I said. 'Shhh' she said, 'don't think about that now, just have a good sleep tonight. I'll be back first thing in the morning.'

I wanted to protest about the drip again but I couldn't get the words out. I hadn't been lying about being tired; I was utterly exhausted. My eyelids were heavy and dragged themselves shut as I slid into oblivion, which was exactly where I wanted to be.

27

JENNA

'Do you want another drink?' Dad and I had been sitting for ages in the hospital canteen, waiting for Mum to come down.

I shook my head. 'I want to go home.'

'I'm sure Mum won't be long now' he said, glancing up at the clock. It was getting late. I'd had so many hot chocolates but that wasn't the only thing making me feel sick. I was itching to get my school uniform off and shower this horrible day away.

A classical tune tinkled somewhere underneath the table. Dad pulled his mobile out of his pocket. 'Helen' I heard him say. 'Yes, thanks, that's great. If you could keep her overnight that would really help. Yes, she's stabilised now. We're just waiting for Jean. Yes, Jenna's ok, she's here with me now. OK, bye.' He snapped his phone shut. 'Helen's ok to look after Lily tonight.'

'She'll love that. Charlie will spoil her rotten. What has Helen told her?'

'Not a lot. I don't think she's that curious.'

'You need to talk to her Dad – she was really upset the

other day. She doesn't understand why Leila behaves as she does.'

Dad sighed. 'That makes two of us.'

We sat in silence until a clip clopping noise made me look round. It was Mum in her heels, heading towards us. She looked shattered. Dad got up and put his arms around her.

'Let's get out of here' she said. 'I'm sick of this place.'

Dad drove us back. 'I'm hungry, Mum' I said. It was hours ago since Mary and I had shared our sandwiches. 'Let's stop off at the fish and chip shop' said Dad. 'Comfort food – that's what we need.'

We sat in the back of the car, munching our food. The satisfying aroma of chips and vinegar filled the air.

'She's not telling the whole truth,' Mum said. 'I don't think PC Ellis believed her either. There's something she's not saying. It might help if you go and see her tomorrow, Jenna' she said, swivelling round in her seat to look at me. 'Perhaps she might talk to you?'

I nodded, wiping my mouth with the back of my hand, finishing off the last chip. I screwed the newspaper wrapping up into a ball. 'I'll try, but don't get your hopes up. She doesn't tell me much these days.' I squeezed the newspaper into a ball, kneading it with my hands. 'I want my old sister back.'

'I've arranged for the Psychologist from the Eating Disorders Unit to go and see her tomorrow – you know it would have been her appointment on Friday anyway. Her reaction to that drip frightened me – she would have ripped it out if she could have. I don't think we can deal with this at home any more. They may be able to transfer her in the next couple of days, but Leila doesn't know that yet, obviously.'

It was dark by the time Dad pulled up outside out house. The lights were out next door so Mum didn't bother to go in and check on Lily. I went straight up to bed, Leila's empty bed a sobering reminder of her absence.

Sleep eluded me. After a couple of hours I went downstairs and got myself a glass of cold water. I couldn't stop thinking about Leila and Kelsey and the blade. I had a horrible suspicion about where it had come from. I needed to ask Leila some questions – but how could I make her answer them?

I got up early and Dad and I sat in the kitchen and ate our cereal together. He had left Mum asleep as Helen had taken Lily to school. The news was on in the background and I was half listening to a story about rising bread prices. It was funny how things carried on regardless, while our family was hanging on a knife edge – literally.

'Come on Dad' I said impatiently. 'Let's get going.'

The hospital was in full flow when Dad dropped me off. I normally quite liked the hustle and bustle of hospitals and was considering a career in medicine. I enjoyed maths and science and I really liked looking after people. Today, however, I didn't pay much attention. I went up the stairs two at a time as there was a queue at the lifts which included two people being taken upstairs on trolleys. I thought of my classmates, they would be coming out of assembly now. For a second I wished I were back at school with them.

Leila was on a female ward on the third floor and I stopped in the doorway to catch my breath before I went in. I looked for Leila. There were six beds with elderly patients in them. I must have got the wrong ward. I was about to turn back when the patient in the far bed by the window caught my eye. My stomach lurched. It was Leila. Her frail figure and drawn face had aged her so much I hadn't recognised her. I swallowed hard. She was sitting up in bed and a nurse was helping her to eat some breakfast. Leila was glaring at the plate which contained a couple of slices of toast and jam. My stomach rumbled. The nurse got up when I arrived. 'I've been trying to get her to eat but she says she's not hungry. You look as if you could do with a good breakfast, dear.'

'I don't want it' shouted Leila, 'why won't anybody listen to me?' The old lady in the bed opposite woke up with a start. Leila kicked her legs up in the bed deliberately forcing the plate of toast to catapult onto the floor.

'Leila' I hissed, horrified. The old lady opposite started cackling loudly, opening her toothless mouth wide. 'What's got into you?' I picked up the toast which of course had landed sticky side down on the floor and located the plate which had rolled under the bed. At least it hadn't smashed. The nurse came back with some cleaning materials and motioned to me to sit back down with Leila.

'You can't behave like that!' Leila slumped down in the bed and I felt a pang of pity for her. She looked so uncomfortable. I had an idea. I went and had a word with the nurse, explaining that I needed to talk to Leila somewhere more private. Before I knew it, she had fetched a wheelchair and I was wheeling Leila off along the corridor, drip in tow.

'Just get me out of here' groaned Leila, but the best I could manage was a day room at the end of the corridor. It wasn't great, but it was empty and there was a good view of the grounds from here so we sat in front of the large window and some fresh air blew in on us through the open window.

'How's your arm?' I asked. 'It hurts like hell' she said. 'It kept me awake at night, that and the batty old lady in the bed opposite. They're going to move me onto the children's ward if I have to stay any longer, but there was no room when I came in. That's got to be better than here.'

'What happened, Lee?' I asked her. 'I've been awake all night trying to work it out. Did Kelsey attack you?'

Leila didn't reply, she stared straight ahead out of the window, but her face twitched up and down.

'Did you take that blade into school?'

'No way!' Her eyes flashed angrily at me. 'How can you think that?'

'Well Kelsey said it wasn't hers – are you saying it was? If it was she will be excluded. This is serious stuff. One of you isn't telling the truth.'

'And you think that's me. Thanks a lot.'

'No. I don't know. I just want you to be clear. You haven't been well and…'

'Look, drop it. I can't remember ok.'

We both sat staring out of the window for a while. If she didn't want to talk to me, I wasn't going to force her, but I needed to know what had happened.

28

LEILA

The hospital was hideous at night. The bright lights from the corridor outside meant that it never got dark, and the old lady in the bed opposite simply would not go to sleep. She kept shouting out in her sleep and after a few hours of that I wanted to go and bash her over the head so that I could get some peace and quiet.

At about ten o clock the next day I had an appointment with Dora, the psychologist from the Eating Disorders Unit, who I had been scheduled to see the previous Friday before the accident had put a stop to that. I was taken down to a different part of the hospital, which was a lot quieter and brighter than the ward where I was.

'Come in' she said, smiling. The nurse wheeled me in then went out and shut the door. 'My name's Dora' she said and reached for my hand. Her skin was warm and soft. She was about fifty, with pale blonde hair cut into a neat bob. She was small and round in a motherly kind of way. She was wearing a dark blue dress with a large necklace to match and patent pointed shoes with kitten heels.

'I'm pleased to meet you Leila' she said. 'I've heard all about you. I'm hoping that I'll be able to move you out of that noisy ward. Would you like that?'

I nodded. The Voice had warned me last night not to trust anyone but I couldn't help warming to her. She had a kind face and a lovely smile and straight away I felt safe.

'How is your arm?' she asked.

'It's not hurting as much now 'I said, looking down at the bandage.

'And how is everything else?'

'They've taken the drip out.' I said.

'And does that make you feel better?'

'It terrified me.'

'Why?'

'I couldn't control what was going into my body. I couldn't stand it. I wanted to pull it out.'

'What do you think it was doing to you?'

'Putting sugar into me. Making me fat.'

'What's wrong with being fat?'

I stared at her. Surely it was obvious. Nobody wanted to be fat.

'I don't want to talk about it.'

'Ok.' She wrote something down on her pad. 'Can you tell me about your family?'

I told her about Dad and Jenna and Lily.

'What about Mum?' she asked. Why did she ask the wrong questions?

'It's difficult.' I said.

'Try me.'

'We argue a lot. She doesn't understand me. Jenna and Lily are good. I'm different to them and she doesn't get it. Dad gets it – a bit.'

'How do you get on with your sisters?'

'Lily's annoying, but only because she's little. Jenna's great. We share a bedroom and we talk a lot. Well, we used to.'

'What's changed?' I thought about it.

'Me.'

'Do you know why you've changed?'

My ear started buzzing. I looked at Dora. Behind her chair a large shadow loomed on the wall. I could see it clearly this time. It was massive. It was me. I gasped.

'Leila what is it?'

I shook my head. My hands shook. My whole body shook.

'Leila? Tell me. I can help you.'

Could I trust her? Could she make it go away? 'It's....' The face on the shadow opened its lipstick red mouth and roared inside my head.

'It's nothing.' I said.

'Ok' she said. 'Tell me about school.'

That was easier. I told her about maths and how it worried me that I was going to fail my exams. I told her about Cherry and Samia. Talking about Samia made me smile.

'It's nice to see you smile' she said. 'You look very serious and worried most of the time.'

'I never used to be like this' I told her.

'Do you think you are ready for a change?' she asked. I thought about it. The last few weeks had been horrible. I was dizzy, cold, depressed. I was exhausted and losing my friends. And then there was The Voice... I shuddered.

'Leila?'

I looked up at Dora with tears in my eyes. 'Yes' I answered. 'But I'm scared that I'm not strong enough to fight it.'

'Listen Leila' said Dora. 'I can see that you are frightened of something.' She took my hands. 'I can help you; I can make the demons in your head go away.'

I was shocked. How did she know? Maybe she could help me after all.

'I think it would help you to move into the unit here for a little while.' I shook my head, dismayed. She got up and came and sat down next to me, putting her arm around me. She smelt nice, flowery. 'All you have to do is concentrate on getting better. You will have an appointment with me every day and we can try and work out what caused you to reach the point where you are today. You will also see a nutritionist, who will plan out your meals with you, with the aim at getting some of your strength back. Does that sound like a plan?'

I thought about it. I could do with a break from my life. I nodded.

'Good' she said. 'I'll take you back down now and we can get you moved as soon as possible. I'm sure you've had enough of those old ladies, haven't you?' She winked at me as she said that. 'Oh, one last thing' she said. 'I want you to write down everything we talk about and it might help you remember what led up to the fight you had at school. I think it will help you.'

'What about my exams?'

'Don't worry about that, we'll arrange for some school work to be sent over for you. We don't want you getting behind now do we; otherwise your mum will be after me.' Her twinkly eyes were reassuring and I felt calmer than I had done in ages. As we went back downstairs in the lift, my head was spinning, but she had given me a glimmer of hope. I would put my trust in Dora and start fighting. Fighting to get my life back.

29

JENNA

Mary and I were sitting with Samia and Cherry in Café Blanco. Samia had rung me and suggested meeting up and I had brought Mary along for moral support as I didn't know Leila's friends very well. I told them what had happened with PC Ellis. I didn't tell them my own theories about what had happened; I wasn't even sure myself at this point. I did tell them however that none of us entirely believed Leila when she said that it wasn't her blade. That way I could see if any of the others were thinking along the same lines as I was.

'Why would she have a razor blade though?' asked Cherry. 'I suppose she does have all sorts of strange things in her pencil case. Tweezers, eyeliner, that kind of thing, the sort of stuff you normally put in a makeup bag. Maybe it was for an art project?'

'I guess if it is her blade she's probably too frightened to say anything in case she gets kicked out of school' pondered Cherry. 'What's happening with Kelsey anyway?'

'She's been suspended from school while the investigation is on. I suppose if Leila wasn't in hospital she would have been suspended too, until they find out what really happened.' I told them.

Mary looked deep in thought. 'Are you sure Leila hasn't lost her memory? Maybe she bumped her head when she fainted?' she asked. I didn't think that was the case at all. The nurses had said there was no physical reason for loss of memory although the shock of the trauma could have had something to do with it.

'Do you know when Leila will be coming home?' asked Cherry. 'We'll go and visit her tomorrow if she's still there.'

Samia nodded in agreement. 'I need to see her' she said. 'I feel terrible because the last time I saw her we parted on bad terms.' She told us about her invitation to Leila to go to McDonald's to meet George. 'It was a stupid thing to suggest, I should have realised how she would react. I just wanted it to be like old times when we used to hang out and have fun. I was going to catch up with her at school to talk about it but I never got the chance.' She looked really upset and Cherry squeezed her arm.

'Don't beat yourself up Sami' she said. 'It's so hard to know what to do for the best. Don't laugh, but I was thinking of writing in to Bliss magazine for some advice.' She shook her head in bewilderment, her copper curls bouncing from side to side.

'Nothing's been decided yet, but I think she'll still be in there tomorrow.' I told them. 'She'd love for you to visit.'

'Let's go and buy her a present' said Cherry to Samia. 'We can take it in tomorrow.'

I was more open with Mary after they'd gone.

'Leila's probably going to be moved into the Eating Disorders Unit. I didn't tell the others as Leila doesn't know yet.'

'That's good isn't it?'

'Yes. I hope so.'

'Will you be at school next week, Jenna?' she asked.

'I don't know' I said. 'I'm not sure I can face it, to be honest. I can't stand all the gossip.'

'I don't blame you. I can get work for you if your mum is worried about that.'

'Thanks.'

I watched her walk off in the opposite direction. I was confused. I didn't like the idea of Leila being on a psychiatric ward, which was where the Eating Disorders Unit was, but she needed help and I hated to admit it, but it was easier at home without her.

Mary rang me the following night.

'OMG.' She sounded breathless. Mary spoke even faster when she was excited. 'It's a good job you're not at school,' she said. 'The Fight' is what it's now known as and everybody is talking about it. It even has its own Facebook page. Can you believe that?'

I switched my phone onto speaker and pulled my laptop to me with my other hand, logging onto Facebook.'

'What are you doing?' Mary asked. 'There's no point looking at Facebook because it's been taken off already. The Head went mad and called a special assembly. We got to miss maths though, so that was a result. Oh I'm sorry, that sounded harsh.'

'What did it say on Facebook?'

'I don't think I should tell you.'

'Mary, come on.'

'Well it was stupid stuff like Kelsey was trying to kill Leila because she was jealous of her being thin.'

'Who could be jealous of Leila? She's a mess.'

'She's thin, though. Who doesn't want to be thin these days?'

She had a point.

'What did the Head say?'

'She said that it was an on-going investigation and that we shouldn't talk about it. As if! She said PC Ellis did not need to be wasting her time looking at Facebook stuff as well as everything else. I'm so glad you're not at school, Jen. You would hate it.'

'I told Mum I'm not going back yet. I can't handle it.'

'Have you seen Leila? Do you know what happened? Was Kelsey attacking her?'

'I don't know' I said. 'She won't talk about it.'

I couldn't even share my suspicions with Mary. When I had been researching eating disorders with Charlie, I had found out that a lot of young people affected also self-harm. Last night it had suddenly occurred to me. Leila had started having lots of baths – something she had never done before, always preferring showers. I believed her that she wasn't vomiting, but she always seemed very distracted and looked washed out when she came out of the bathroom.

That could be an explanation for what had happened. Leila was the only person I could ask and that was too difficult, but what if I was wrong? She would never forgive me.

Lily had asked me when Leila was coming home. 'I don't know' I had said, 'hopefully soon.' But what if I was right and she ended up going to prison for having a weapon? I had to keep my mouth shut.

30

LEILA

It felt strange to be on my own. I had been moved to a small room, painted off white, with a bed and a cupboard and a huge window which looked out onto the hospital grounds. I was thrilled about the window, as it was still sunny out and the leaves were that gorgeous red brown and yellow which comes with autumn. Autumn had always been my favourite season. The bathroom was along the corridor and I was only allowed to use it under supervision until I had built up some privileges. I was determined to make a go of things and the first thing I did was note down everything that Dora had said in my journal. Writing helped clarify my mind.

The nutritionist came to visit me on the afternoon that I arrived. She was a young Asian woman called Ayesha; so young in fact that she can't have been that much older than me. She was really bubbly and chatty, which helped when we started going through the menus.

'The amount of food that you need to eat is non-negotiable' she said, 'but you get a certain amount of choice. Go through them now and tick the options that you prefer.'

I looked at the sheets she handed me. The black lettering swam in front of me. 'It's too hard.' I said. 'Having to choose to eat, I don't know if I can.'

'Don't think about it. Think of food as medicine that you need to take three times a day.'

'I feel so greedy' I said.

'Leila' she said. 'You're keeping yourself alive. Missing a meal or cheating is sabotaging yourself and your recovery. Just do it. The more you eat regular meals the less of an issue it will be as your body gets out of the danger zone. One day you'll realise you're doing it without thinking.'

'I can't imagine that' I said, but I started to find things on the list to tick off and before I knew it I had selected my meals for the next week. Was I really going to eat all that?

'Don't think about it' she repeated, 'I can see you're getting anxious again. You'll be able to talk to Dora about your worries when you see her. Talk as much as you can – secrets need to be out in the open in here. Tell me what you are thinking now.'

'I want to go and look all these meals up on the internet now, see what's in them.'

'Why do you think there is no internet access in here?'

The rules had been explained to me on admission. I had access to a mobile phone (without internet) for an hour each evening. Visitor privileges would change according to my progress. There was a television in the day room – that was about it for mod cons. I would miss PerfectlyThin but Kate had given me her mobile number. I had never used it, but I hadn't needed to. I certainly did now. She had been in hospital before and would know what it was like. I would get in touch with her later on. I didn't think Ayesha would approve somehow, but one call couldn't hurt, surely?

I was resting late one afternoon after I had been in my room for a few days when the nurse came in and told me I had a visitor, a friend from school. I was surprised as Samia and Cherry had only been in the day before. The door to my room had to be kept ajar, it was one of the rules, but I liked hearing what was going on around me. I looked up as I heard heavy footsteps approaching and nearly fell out of bed when I saw Kelsey standing in the doorway. She was the last person I had expected to visit.

'Can I come in?' she said. I nodded, in a state of shock. I wasn't sure that I wanted to see her but it looked like I didn't have a choice. She sat in the visitor's armchair and put her bag and umbrella down on the floor. I looked at her properly for the first time. Kelsey was really overweight. She was wearing a long black skirt and a shapeless purple t-shirt, which must have been at least extra-large. It covered her bum and thighs and she kept pulling it down self-consciously. I had hardly ever seen her out of uniform. Her chestnut brown hair was shoulder length, but unwashed looking. There was an air of defeat about her and she avoided my eyes.

'What are you doing here?' I asked. 'Are you even supposed to be here?'

She shrugged her shoulders. 'Mum thinks I'm at school. She doesn't really care what I do. I just came up the stairs following the signs for Montreal ward. Nobody stopped me. If they ask me to leave I will. Do you want me to leave?'

I didn't know what to say. I wasn't particularly comfortable with her being there and I was a little bit scared. She could get me in a lot of trouble. She shifted around in her chair and started chewing her thumb. It was painful.

'Why are you here?' I asked again.

She looked a bit taken aback, and then really embarrassed. She blushed deep red. What on earth was the matter with her? An uncomfortable silence stretched between us. Her voice was very quiet when she suddenly started speaking.

'I feel so bad about what happened. I didn't mean to get you into trouble, I swear.' She was as in as much trouble if not more than I was, so her words surprised me. I had expected her to be aggressive, especially as I hadn't confessed to owning the blade. Why wasn't she angry with me?

'What do you mean?' I said. She sat upright, steeling herself for something and then the words came tumbling out of her mouth. 'I hate school. I hate living here. Where we used to live I had friends, but nobody likes me here. I don't blame them. Who wants a fat ugly loser as a friend?' That sounded familiar. 'You remind me of my friend Penny.' She sighed. 'I'm probably not making much sense.'

She was right. She was freaking me out.

'When you left early that lunchtime I saw it as a chance to be able to speak to you on your own.'

'Who is Penny? I don't get what you're on about. Why would you want to talk to me? No offence, but we're not friends.'

She looked uncomfortable. 'I knew you wouldn't understand. I was worried about you. Especially when... when...' Her voice faltered then she rushed the last bit of the sentence out, '....when you started losing weight. That's what happened to Penny. I find it so hard to lose weight; I wanted to know how you did it.'

'What do you mean "that's what happened to Penny?"'

'She was really ill. I could see you going the same way.' A look of angst flickered across her face. 'I don't like my body in

164

the same way that you don't like yours. I can see what you are doing is wrong but at the same time I want to be able to do it too. It was the same with Penny. I wanted to help her but I also wished I had her will power.' She shook her head. 'Stupid I know, but that's me all over.'

'So was Penny in the same class as you at school?'

Kelsey looked flustered. 'No' she said, 'not exactly.'

What on earth did that mean?

A shadow flickered across her eyes. For a split second she looked angry. What wasn't she telling me?

'Forget I said anything. It was a stupid idea to visit. The reason I came here is to tell you that I have spoken to PC Ellis and I told her I don't know where the weapon came from. I said I thought it was probably part of your art stuff. The main thing is I said it was an accident. I know we haven't always seen eye to eye and we had that stupid argument in Café Blanco, but you do need me. I don't want to get you into trouble. In fact, Mum's taking me out of that school anyway so I can take the blame if you want, I don't really care.'

She wasn't making sense to me. Why would she offer to do that? Why wasn't she more curious about the blade? Did she really think it was all an accident? I still didn't trust her. I looked at her. She was looking really dejected, her head bowed over her knees, her eyes cast down to the floor. I felt a pang of sympathy for her. It must be horrid to have no friends and to hate school so much. Then I remembered that she had triggered the chain of events that led to me being put in hospital, by following me into the toilet. I would not feel sorry for her, she was trouble.

Suddenly she stood up. 'I shouldn't have come' she said. 'I can see you're annoyed. But I meant what I said; I won't tell anyone what happened.' She picked up her bag and was gone before I had a chance to react. What was all that about? I wished I could call her back, but I had probably scared her off for good now.

31

JENNA

Charlie and I were sitting on the swings in the park. He was still in his school uniform as I had arranged to meet him on his way home from school, having been cooped up indoors all day. We were going to chill out for a bit, then go into town for a burger. It had been a sunny day and it was still warm in the early evening. I had been trying to work out what to do since I woke up this morning; I was going round in circles. I needed Charlie's advice, but how could I not betray Leila? I needed the right words, but I couldn't work out what they were.

'Are you alright Jenna?' Charlie asked. 'You seem miles away. Is everything ok?'

'Not really' I said, 'but it's a bit difficult. I want to ask your advice without telling you exactly what it's about.'

'Ok...' said Charlie, looking a little puzzled. 'But you know you can trust me. I'm not going to tell anyone; we don't even go to the same school.'

I thought about how I could make him understand. 'It would feel like a betrayal' I said. 'I'm only speculating really and if I get it wrong the less people that know about it the better.'

'Isn't that a bit unfair on me?' asked Charlie, looking upset.

I'd never seen him like that before. 'What do you mean?' I asked.

'Well, keeping me in the dark when you know you can trust me?'

'I do trust you' I replied 'but this isn't something I can share.'

'Why not?' he asked. I didn't know what to say. Not wanting to voice my suspicions about Leila in case I was wrong seemed really important to me. An awkward, uncomfortable silence stretched between us. I'd never felt like this with Charlie before.

'You need to talk to someone Jenna, someone you can trust. I always thought that was me, but obviously I was wrong.' He jumped up off the swing. 'I'm going home. See you later.' With that he made off dejectedly towards the park gate, his head hanging down.

I got up off the swing, my inertia turning into despair. How could he get me so wrong? I thought about what he had said as I wandered aimlessly across the park, not really caring where I was going. Had I taken him for granted? He must have known that I really liked him. Why would I spend so much time with him otherwise? Maybe he was getting sick of Leila and her problems. I know I was.

I was so engrossed in my thoughts that I wasn't taking any notice of my surroundings until I realised that somebody was calling my name. Startled I looked in the direction that the sound was coming from. I didn't recognise the voice at first until I caught sight of Kara and Stacey, two girls from my year at school. Kara was one of the 'In' girls; really popular and totally into boys and fashion. I quite liked her, but she was only in one of my lessons and I thought I was way too nerdy for her to pay much attention to me. They were seated on the floor leaning against a tree. It was quite secluded in this part of the park. I didn't usually come this way on my own but I had been so distracted that I hadn't been looking where I was going.

'We saw you earlier with your boyfriend' said Kara. 'He looks cute.'

'He's not my boyfriend' I scowled. I didn't want to think about Charlie at the moment.

'Have you had a row?' asked Stacey. Stacey and I had been at primary school together, but our paths hadn't crossed much at Stenfield Academy. We'd always got on ok though and her mum was quite friendly with mine.

'Sit down' said Kara. 'We were just about to have a picnic', she said giggling, 'Why don't you join us?'

I didn't know what she meant until Stacey pulled a bottle of vodka out of her bag and took a swig. 'Want some?' she asked.

I was completely out of my comfort zone. First there was the row with Charlie, now this. What the hell I thought, I could do with the distraction. I sat down next to Stacey. My phone buzzed in my pocket and I took it out and turned it off and threw it to the bottom of my bag. Stacey handed me the bottle and I took a swig. The bitter liquid hit the back of my throat and made me cough. Kara laughed.

'Take it easy' she said, 'have some lemonade with it.' She took a huge plastic bottle of lemonade and some paper cups out of her bag. 'We're quite civilised you know.'

'We've even got some crisps' said Stacey, producing a supermarkets own brand family sized pack and we all laughed. Stacey poured me a cupful of lemonade with a generous amount of vodka. I had tried wine before at home once, it was disgusting. This didn't taste too bad. Best of all I liked the way it made me relax.

'Did you see Mrs Lyons in assembly today? She was checking people's shoes. She is so weird.' She stood up and mimicked Mrs Lyons mincing up and down the hall. Her voice was spot on. Kara and I giggled helplessly. This was just what I needed. The row with Charlie had been the last straw. I had been so fed up at home lately, I was sick of Leila and all the attention she got and I wished she'd just shut up and eat. I was fed up of being so understanding. School was bad enough before Leila decided to throw us all into the spotlight. Thinking about school made me remember the razor blade and my suspicions. I shivered. I put it out of my mind and took another swig of vodka. Tonight I was going to be different. I was finally letting my hair down.

I don't know how long we were there for but Mum thought I was out with Charlie anyway. We suddenly realised the park might close and decided to make a move. The empty vodka bottle had been cast aside; the lemonade was all gone when Kara announced that she was getting cold. I wasn't cold at all despite not having a jacket; I felt warm and fuzzy inside. When I stood up the trees lurched around my head and I grabbed hold of Kara to balance myself. Stacey tripped up and stared giggling hysterically. Once everything stopped spinning I felt a bit better and arm in arm we staggered over to the park gates. Kara and Stacey insisted on walking me home as I only lived around the corner. We were just coming up to the top of my road when the queasiness returned and I knew I was going to be sick. I wrenched my arm away from Stacey and threw up violently in the gutter. Stacey was still giggling but Kara held my hair back and gave me some tissues. I felt terrible but the vomiting and the cold air made me feel a bit better. I needed to get into the house without Mum seeing me.

I managed to persuade Stacey and Kara to leave me at the end of my street as I didn't want Stacey making a racket outside my house and drawing Mum's attention to us. Besides, she thought I was out with Charlie. The thought of Charlie made me feel irritated again. I took a deep breath and let myself into the house with my key.

'Is that you Jenna?' I heard Dad call out from the living room. I could hear the sound of television in the background.

'Yes Dad' I called, 'I'm desperate for the loo' and went upstairs as quickly as I could manage. 'Desperate' was hard to get my tongue round and the bannisters didn't quite seem to be in the right place. In the bathroom I pressed my forehead against the cold white tiles. Soothed, I slowly drank a large glass of water. I got changed into my dressing gown, then went downstairs to the kitchen to make myself a cup of hot chocolate. The thought of chocolate made me gag again and I steadied myself against the wall. I didn't want Mum to be suspicious, so I needed to follow my usual routine.

My brain was still feeling weird, and I realised I hadn't eaten since lunchtime. Just like my sister. Maybe I was turning into her. Good, I thought. I was sick of goody two shoes Jenna. I picked the milk bottle up to put back in the fridge but somehow it slipped through my fingers and dropped onto the floor with an almighty crash. There was glass everywhere. I stood looking at it, feeling really strange. How had that happened? For some reason the sight of my feet covered in milk struck me as funny and I started to giggle uncontrollably.

Mum came rushing into the kitchen. 'What on earth was that?' she asked, looking at me incredulously. 'Well don't just stand there, Jenna. What on earth is the matter with you?'

'Who's Jenna?' I said which made me laugh even more.

Mum came over and seized me by the shoulders. Her feet crunched on the glass shards on the floor. 'Jenna? Oh no' she said, looking into my eyes. Her face kept slipping in and out of focus. 'You've been drinking haven't you? Will!' she shouted, 'Come here now!'

Dad rushed in and looked at the floor, then at Mum and me standing in the middle of the carnage. 'What on earth?' he asked.

'She's been drinking' Mum said furiously. 'Wait till I see Charlie. I knew he was too old for you.' Suddenly everything was too much and I collapsed onto Mum and burst into tears.

'I wasn't with Charlie' I sobbed, 'We had a row. I never want to speak to him again.'

Dad took charge of the situation. 'Take her up to bed, Jean' he said. 'I'll sort this lot out.' He sounded pretty grim. 'We need to talk to you young lady, but it can wait until the morning when you're in a better state. I'm shocked at you Jenna, I really am.'

Mum took me upstairs and helped me into bed. I was scared and upset and didn't say a word. I left my phone turned off on the bedroom floor, under a heap of clothes. I didn't want to know whether Charlie had been in touch. Right then I wanted to forget he ever existed.

32

LEILA

I had been on the unit for a week now and I was starting to struggle. For the first weekend here the normal regulations of the unit had not applied as I'd moved in under special circumstances. Since Monday they had swung into place with a vengeance and I was no longer allowed visitors during week days until I had put on six kilos in weight. Dora had explained that I should not have any external distractions as I had enough going on at the moment as it was. I wasn't completely free of visitors as I'd had a couple of visits from PC Ellis and Mrs Paris had brought in some work for me; highly embarrassing entertaining my Head of Year in a hospital bed wearing a nightdress.

I was still allowed my phone for an hour in the evening so I had sent Kate a message as soon as I got the chance. When I switched my phone on the next night she had sent me three messages. She was full of sympathy and gave me a few tips on how to handle the nurses. It cheered me up initially, but then I realised that she was assuming I wanted to lose weight still. I hadn't told her that I was trying to get better. Somehow, I didn't think she'd be impressed.

I brought up the subject of Kate at my next meeting with Dora.

'Where did you meet her?' she asked.

'Online. It's a great website called PerfectlyThin. I've got a few friends on there. The girls I meet hate their bodies like I do. I find talking to them helps. I miss them now that I'm in here.'

Dora scribbled in her notebook.

'What would they have to say about you being in here? Do you think they would encourage you to get better?'

I thought of Kate's text telling me not to trust the staff. I looked down at my hands.

'Have you met up with anyone from the site?'

I shook my head. 'But I will. I've joined a local group.'

She sighed.

'These sites are dangerous, Leila. You have no idea who these people really are.'

'Yes, I do. I've seen photos and we chat about where we live and our schools and stuff. What are you trying to say?'

'I think you know what I'm telling you. I know about PerfectlyThin and several other similar sites. They are known as ProAna sites; they encourage girls with anorexia to lose weight and are very dangerous. It's best to avoid them altogether.'

'I don't see why' I said, sulkily. 'Can't I just keep in touch with Kate?'

'Will she support you while you are in here and encourage you to put on weight and rest?'

I couldn't see that happening. I shook my head. I realised what she was getting at.

'It won't be easy Leila. None of this is easy. But if you can talk about everything with me then I can try and help you. I want you to promise me you won't have any more contact with any of these girls that you have met online.'

Back in my room the nurse was waiting with my morning snack. It was a cup of hot chocolate and a Kit Kat. Every time I had to eat now I held Ayesha's words in my mind about treating food like medicine. It helped a lot.

'Well done Leila' the nurse said as she cleared up the tray, 'You're trying hard, I can see that. I'll be back at lunchtime. Have a rest now.'

I was pleased with myself. I couldn't wait to tell Jenna that I'd eaten a whole Kit Kat.

I lay back on my bed, fixing my eyes on the painting on the opposite wall. It was an abstract piece, made up of long thin shapes. I decided to get my diary out and write down today's achievements. Maybe it wasn't a good idea to contact Kate, it just confused me. As I reached across to my bedside table to get my diary a loud buzzing filled my head. A movement on the wall caught my eye. The central shape in the painting was thickening and moving in 3D fashion towards me. There was no doubt it was a person, a person coming towards me with outstretched arms. I flinched, recoiling back towards the wall. The shape trembled like a jelly, threatening to envelop me.

So you've given up, just like that?

The Voice. It hadn't been this loud since the day in the park.

Can't you see what's in front of you? Is this what you want to look like? Because you will, if you let them fool you

175

I closed my eyes, willing the shape to go away. I peered through my eyelashes. The shape taunted me, hovering in front of the painting. I could see the face clearly now, the features were familiar, like looking in a mirror. I gasped in horror; the shadow was me! The Voice was showing me what I looked like.It was laughing now, a harsh sound that chilled my blood. I clutched my head in my hands to try and shake it out. All of a sudden there was silence inside and out. It had gone. I lay back on the bed, my heart racing. How was I going to beat that? I shut my eyes and lay still until the tremors had stilled. I breathed deeply, calming myself down. Clattering noises from trolleys rattling down the corridor heralded the start of lunch. I remembered my earlier triumph at eating a KitKat. The picture was back to normal now. I glared at it. I would conquer this.

That afternoon in the school room our tutor Wendy was full of enthusiasm. Her energy contrasted with my mental exhaustion. The earlier encounter with The Voice had drained me. Writing the incident down had helped, but I still had an unbearable tension tugging at my insides. I hadn't felt this wound up since that fateful day at school. I was supposed to be working on a collage using images from magazines. My eyes fell on the craft knife laid on the table in front of me, tempting me. Wendy had her back to me as she helped another patient choose her images. In a trice I had the craft knife hidden in the pocket of my skirt. Calmly, I replaced it with another knife from the rack. Cutting myself was the only thing in my head now.

I always had a shower before my evening meal so that was my opportunity. While the water was cascading over me I cut deeply into the top of my leg. I had taken a pile of J cloths out of the school room so I could use them to clean up after myself without soiling the towels. The relief I felt was overwhelming. Not only had I made progress with my food but I had found an outlet for my feelings. I lay on my bed afterwards, the agitation temporarily stilled. As the corridors quietened and night settled in I finally drifted off into a restless sleep.

33

JENNA

I woke up the next morning feeling terrible. At first I couldn't work out why my head was pulsing and my mouth felt as if I'd swallowed a sheet of sandpaper. Slowly, horrible memories from last night started drifting into my mind. What on earth had I done? Parts of my memory were blurred, but I recalled being in the park with Stacey and Kara and then the bottle of milk dropping on the floor in the kitchen and Mum being mad at me. Then I remembered Charlie and groaned. I went to sit up to get my phone but pain seared through my head. Sudden movements were out of the question. Gingerly, I eased myself into a sitting position and slowly reached down to the floor for my bag. I fumbled around for my phone. The slightest movement felt inordinately complicated to achieve.

There were five missed calls from Charlie and one text message:

Call me, PLEASE. C xxx

I was relieved he had been in touch and wasn't going to ignore me forever. I didn't often row with Leila but when I did she usually stopped speaking to me for at least a day and I had feared he would do the same. He would be horrified if he knew what I had done. Maybe I wouldn't tell him but then that might drive him further away. My memory of the latter part of the evening was hazy but the scenes with Charlie flashed over and over in my mind. Despite being upset he had still managed to give me some good advice. I did need to talk to someone but there was no way I would talk to Mum. Leila would never forgive me if she found out.

I put my dressing gown and teddy bear slippers on and padded downstairs, my legs still a bit wobbly. I was shocked to see that it was nearly midday. I was supposed to have been back at school. Mum was sitting in the kitchen, reading the newspaper. She started when I went in and glanced up at the clock.

'Jenna, darling, how are you feeling?' She was being nice; I wasn't expecting that.

'Not good. Mum I'm so sorry.' I sat down on the bar stool next to her and put my head in my hands. 'Aren't you working today?' It was Wednesday, and usually Mum worked the afternoon shift.

'I've taken the afternoon off. I wanted to keep an eye on you and we need to have a talk. What you did last night was wrong, very wrong, but it was totally out of character and nothing has been very normal around here lately, has it? Leila being ill has taken up all of mine and Dad's attention and perhaps we've been neglecting you. I'm really sorry, darling. You must have been feeling pretty bad to do what you did last night. I am right, aren't I? This was a first wasn't it? Or has it happened before and I just haven't noticed?'

'No Mum, of course not' I said. 'I don't know what came over me. I had an argument with Charlie and he left me in the park. I bumped into Kara and Stacey and it just happened. You know I don't hang around with Stacey, we don't see much of each other anymore. And I don't know Kara at all. They were nice though, Mum. I know you don't approve of them because of what's happened, but they didn't force me. I just wanted to do something to forget about everything.'

'I can't ignore the fact that girls your age are going around drinking alcohol. Jenna, you know that. I will be having a word with Stacey's Mum when I see her next.'

'Oh Mum' I wailed, 'that will just make everything worse. They'll probably hate me then.'

'No, they won't' she assured me. 'I'll explain the whole situation to Pat; I just want her to be aware of what her daughter is getting up to. I would expect the same from her.'

I sighed. Yet another problem to add to my growing list of stuff to worry about.

'What did you and Charlie argue about anyway?'

I was silent for a moment, sifting my thoughts into the right order. 'I had something on my mind and I didn't want to tell him about it. He thought I didn't trust him. I do, Mum, but I'm really confused.'

'Can you tell me?' she asked 'Or Dad?'

I shook my head. 'Actually, Mum, I'd like to speak to PC Ellis at school about it.'

Mum looked startled. 'The school Police Officer? Oh Jenna, you didn't get up to anything foolish last night did you?' 'Mum' I said indignantly. 'Don't be ridiculous. It's to do with something that's been happening at school, nothing to do with me.' I was telling her the truth without implicating Leila. I had decided PC Ellis would know what to do.

'Well when you go into school tomorrow you can arrange it then, can't you?' said Mum.

I clenched my fists to pluck up all my courage. 'I'm not going back to school yet, Mum. I can't face it. Not while all this stuff with Leila and Kelsey is going on. I can't concentrate and I'm terrified of what people will say to me.'

Mum looked concerned. 'You can't just stop going to school' she said. 'Maybe a few more days then' she conceded, 'Until you're feeling stronger. What about PC Ellis? Would you like me to see if I can arrange that?'

I frowned. 'I'm not going into school Mum.'

Mum stood up. 'I'll go and phone Mrs Paris, she'll know who I need to get in touch with. I'm sure she could arrange for PC Ellis to visit you here.'

I breathed a sigh of relief. There was no way I was going to set foot in school before I had put my mind at rest. Not until I had sorted out this business with Leila and the blade. I was aware that speaking to PC Ellis may well confirm my worst fears. If my suspicions were right Leila would be in a lot of trouble and, I thought to myself, neither of us may ever be able to set foot in school again.

34

LEILA

I put my pen down. My leg was sore, making it hard to concentrate. I thought back to this morning's conversation with Dora. She could see right through me at times.

'You're doing well, Leila.' She was flicking through my file on her desk. I tried to read the numbers over her shoulder but it was too far away. 'You've reached your target for this week.' I scowled.

'Aren't you pleased?' she sounded surprised. 'Or have you changed your mind about getting better already?'

'No, it's not that. It's hard though, changing the way you think. I really do want this but part of me is still frightened.'

'I understand and you know I am going to help you push that part out of your life forever.'

A silence simmered between us for a few minutes.

'You seem preoccupied, Leila. Are you sure there's nothing on your mind?'

I shook my head, biting my thumbnail. It was hard to lie to her.

I put my notebook back under my pillow and closed my eyes. I must have dropped off to sleep because the next thing I knew someone was calling my name.

'Leila, wake up.'

I opened my eyes reluctant to be pulled out of the dream I had been having and to my surprise found myself face to face with Kelsey.

'What are you doing here?' I asked, surprised. I struggled to sit up, embarrassed.

'I left my umbrella here last time.'

'I think the Nurse has it.' I said. There was a long silence, then Kelsey spoke.

'I wanted to bring you something, but I couldn't decide what. Mum said flowers aren't allowed and I didn't think you'd want grapes or chocolates.' She giggled nervously. 'So I got you some magazines' she said, and pulled a pile of about six different magazines out of her bag. Heat, More, Closer, all my favourite kind full of gossip and lots of skinny celebrities to study.

'Thanks' I said, warily. 'Actually I'm glad you came back' I said. 'It was good of you not to tell on me to PC Ellis and I wanted to say thank you. But I don't understand why you don't want to get me into trouble. I haven't exactly been nice to you, have I?' I hesitated, wondering whether she would take offence about what I was about to say. 'I got the impression there was something you weren't telling me last time, when you started telling me about your friend Penny.'

'You're right' she said. I waited.

'It's about how I met Penny,' she said eventually. 'We didn't go to school together. We…er… we met in hospital. She was in a unit, like this one. Well, it was an adolescent psychiatric unit. I was in there too.'

She was looking down at her hands. I looked questioningly at her. She continued, speaking really fast as if afraid she might change her mind, her eyes fixed on a spot just above my right shoulder.

'I'm a compulsive over eater. I was having a lot of problems and mum couldn't cope. There's only me and mum. I never knew my dad. I was really depressed. Penny and I became friends straight away and we helped each other. She's doing really well now; she's almost up to a normal weight and is back at school. Unlike me, I still haven't lost any weight.' She looked bitter. 'I miss Penny.'

'What school does she go to?' I asked.

'Larksmead' she said.

That explained her obsession with going to that school. It had nothing to do with the fact that it was mixed.

'Surely you can keep in touch? It's not as if you were friends from school anyway is it?'

She shook her head. She started chewing at her hair. I waited for her to reply.

'Her mum didn't want her to stay in touch with anyone she had met at the unit. She didn't understand that we helped each other.'

She was hunched down dejectedly in the chair. Suddenly she sat upright.

'Look' she said determinedly. 'I'm sorry if I alarmed you when I kept turning up where you and your friends were. It was stupid, but I wanted to reach out to you. I could see how unhappy you were.'

Her words surprised me; maybe she wasn't so bad after all.

'There's something else' she added. 'I've got this far so I may as well continue. Please don't be angry, but I think I know why you had the razor blade.' My face darkened. I wasn't expecting this. I was on my guard again. She was the only person who knew for sure that the blade was mine.

'I don't know what you're talking about,' I said. 'Maybe it's time that you went. I don't think we should be speaking to each other anyway. If PC Ellis knew...'

'I haven't talked to anyone else about this.' She was getting agitated now. 'I haven't said it was yours, but I know.' She started unbuttoning her sleeve. 'Trust me' she said. 'I know what you do because I do it too.' She pulled up her sleeve and I gasped. Her arm was completely covered in angry scars, criss-crossing one another, horizontally, diagonally, the skin puckered and red. She was staring at me. 'I'm right aren't I? But I don't think anybody knows that you do it and you want to keep it that way, that's why you won't confess about the knife, even if it means getting me into trouble.'

I looked beseechingly at her.

'It's ok' she said. 'Why do you think I haven't told anyone? That's why Mum had me admitted to the unit where I met Penny, because she couldn't cope with me cutting.' I was shocked to hear her say it out loud. 'I'm much better now and I don't do it anymore' she said, 'That's why you need me, because I understand and I can help you stop.'

My head was reeling. Kelsey looked utterly miserable. 'I've said too much haven't I? Put my big foot straight in it. I always do.' She stood up. 'Listen, forget I ever came here. I won't say anything about the blade. I don't want to go back to that school anyway so it doesn't matter if they think it was mine. I'm sorry I came.'

'Kelsey' I said. 'I need to rest now but ...don't beat yourself up about coming here. It's ok. Come again if you want.' Kelsey's face lit up. 'Really? Are you sure?'

'Yes, I'm sure' I said. I wasn't sure at all. I watched her go, my mind racing. I'd had to ask her to come back to keep her on my side, but how could I avoid getting her into trouble if I didn't own up? I dug my fingernails angrily into the cut on my leg, welcoming the pain as it rocked through me, driving the uncomfortable thoughts out of my mind.

35

JENNA

Mum spoke to Mrs Paris and arranged for me to visit PC Ellis at her base at the local police station in town. I was really nervous about going into a police station but anything was better than school at the moment. Every time I thought about it my insides turned to jelly and I broke into a cold sweat. Mum took me down to the station in the car. She was going to take me into see PC Ellis and then she was heading off to her afternoon shift at the surgery. She had arranged for PC Ellis to take me home afterwards.

Mum and I sat in the reception for about ten minutes, as PC Ellis was on the phone. The reception area was small, with a counter where a young policeman sat behind a screen of glass filling in forms. There were four wooden chairs in a row. Apart from me and Mum there was a young man with a shaved head occupying the third chair, who fidgeted a lot, sighed loudly and swore under his breath every time he looked at the clock. Apart from that it was eerily quiet and I was getting increasingly anxious, wondering whether I was about to make a big show of myself in front of PC Ellis. What if I froze and couldn't speak, like when I had to read aloud in English? The more I thought about it the worse I felt, so that it was actually a relief when I saw the familiar face of PC Ellis smiling at me and holding the door to the area behind the counter open. I'd forgotten how approachable she was.

'Come with me, Jenna' she said. To Mum she added, 'Thanks Mrs Summers. I'll make sure she gets home safely.'

She led me down a narrow corridor, passing doors where people were working, some in police uniform; some surprisingly ordinary in everyday clothes. We went into a small office at the end of the corridor and PC Ellis motioned to me to sit down in the comfy looking chair by the window.

'I'll be with you in a minute' she said 'I just need to finish this report.' She tapped at her keyboard and I made the most of the pause to take in my surroundings. PC Ellis's office was in a really nice spot. She looked out over a field and there was a large apple tree just outside the window. Although the office was small it had a cosy feel to it and I liked the bright posters that livened up the walls. A red coat hung on the back of the door and a pair of gorgeous leather wedge boots stood under the desk. I studied PC Ellis as she typed, trying not to make it too obvious. It was hard to imagine her in normal clothes. She had taken her hat off and placed it on the desk; she had dumped her keys and phone in it as if it were a basket. Her hair was plaited into tight corn rows, which covered her head. She was a statuesque woman; the short sleeves showed off her arms which were taut and muscly. She looked like she worked out to get such definition. It reminded me of Charlie and I felt a pang of anguish. Her crisp short sleeved shirt with her Police number on was gleaming white against her dark brown skin. The police uniform had always alarmed me a little, when I had seen her around school, but now I realised it was just a uniform like I had to wear, a requirement of her job. Her desk was fairly empty apart from a photo of her hugging a little boy; they were both smiling broadly at the camera. I liked the idea that she was a mother to the gorgeous little boy with the tight curls and chubby cheeks in the photograph.

'So Jenna' said PC Ellis, closing her laptop lid. 'How are you? I know you haven't been in school for a bit and that you have been having a difficult time lately. I don't know you very well, but I'm guessing that you're not someone who likes having all this attention focussed on them are you?'

I shook my head and started to relax. She continued 'Do you want to tell me why you are here and I'll see if I can help you?'

She had kind twinkly eyes and a really gentle voice. I thought about Kelsey and why I had come and took all my courage into my hands. I told her everything. How I had been worried about Leila so had done some research on eating disorders and discovered that some anorexics self-harm. How I was terrified when Leila started shutting herself into the bathroom that she was making herself sick again, but after the incident at school I had become suspicious that maybe something else was going on and that she was cutting herself. Finally I told her how I was frightened that she had taken something into school to cut herself with and whatever had happened between her and Kelsey had ended up with Leila getting hurt.

'I don't know Kelsey' I said, 'she is a bit odd. I can't imagine her wanting to hurt Leila. But Leila isn't a bad person either.

She would never have hurt anyone deliberately, but...' I was fighting back tears. 'She would hurt herself.' I swallowed hard. 'But I was so frightened that if I told you and I was right Leila would be expelled from school and put on trial and be sent to prison. And if I was wrong, Leila would never forgive me.'

I burst into tears and PC Ellis put her arm around my shoulders. She waited until I had finished crying and handed me a tissue.

'Jenna' she said. 'Please put all thoughts of prison out of your head. You're a very brave girl and you've done absolutely the right thing. I've talked to Kelsey and I believe her story, but she is hiding something. I think she's covering up for Leila. Did you know she'd been to visit Leila?'

I gasped and shook my head. That didn't make any sense.

'You must get it out of your head that you are betraying Leila in any way. If she is self-harming, then she needs help and you have done the right thing in bringing it to my attention. The hospital staff can check her over without her needing to know your part in it.' Her brown eyes were full of compassion. 'Unfortunately I have had many dealings with troubled students over the years and I had my own ideas about where the blade had come from, although I wasn't sure which of the two of them had brought it in.' She seemed about to add something, then stopped. There was a brief pause.

'I think you're right. I think it's likely that Leila does self- harm. As yet I don't know what happened between those girls, but I'm sure it was a tragic accident. I was giving Leila and Kelsey a bit of breathing space, hoping that one of them would decide to come and tell me the truth, but I think now I need to push Leila a bit.' She rapped her fingers on the desk, obviously trying to work out what to do next.

'Are you going to go and see Leila in hospital?' I asked.

'Yes' she said 'I think I should go down and speak to her.'

'Could I come with you?' I asked. PC Ellis's reaction to my fears had boosted my confidence and I wanted to do something to help. Besides, I really needed to see my sister.

She looked at me thoughtfully. 'Please' I begged. 'I might be able to help and I badly want to see Leila. Visitor privileges are very strict.' A thought occurred to me. 'I'm not trying to get out of school.' I added.

She laughed. 'No I don't believe you are' she said, 'although your mother has had a word with me about that. Somehow, I think if we can sort all this out, you'll soon be feeling very differently about everything.' She stood up. 'I think it's a good idea for you to come to the hospital with me. It might help put your mind at rest. Wait there while I go and see if I can arrange it.' She put her hand on my shoulder as she went past and I let out a sigh of relief. I knew I had done the right thing. Maybe, just maybe, we could sort this whole thing out and I would be able to get my sister back.

36

LEILA

Saturdays were really boring in the unit. I was starting to go a little crazy. My room overlooked a row of shops and a café bordering a small green space where the buses stopped. I spent ages gazing longingly out of the window, watching the people going about their business. I longed for fresh air and freedom. During the week I got to go to the schoolroom which at least gave me something to do. Most of the inpatients were allowed home at weekends, so there were very few of us left, and I wasn't encouraged to mix with the other patients. I had already read the magazines Kelsey had brought me – well, mostly I had looked at the pictures as I still found it difficult to concentrate. It was raining hard outside and that didn't help my mood.

I ate my morning snack in silence. It was getting easier, but still took me forever to get through. I wanted to be left alone and was relieved when finally the nurse took the tray and bustled out of the room, her large backside wobbling as she went. That was why I didn't want to put on weight, I thought vindictively. This was so hard. I pushed the destructive thought away. As I watched her go, a large dark figure shuffled towards me. Kelsey. That was all I needed.

She sat down in the chair. Today she was wearing a long black dress under a black leather coat with buckled biker boots. She looked a lot brighter than last time.

'I've spoken to my mum' she said, wriggling out of her coat which she lay over the back of the chair, 'and I think I've talked her out of moving me to a different school.'

I was surprised. 'I thought you couldn't wait to leave Stenfield Academy?'

'Well not any more' she said, sounding surprised. 'Now that we're friends I need to keep an eye on you. Mum's really pleased for me as it's taken me so long to get to know people.'

'Even though she knows what happened at school?' I didn't think her mum would want her to have anything to do with me.

'She's not bothered about that. She'll do anything for an easy life.' I remembered what Kelsey had said before about her mum not showing much interest in her life.

I chose my words carefully. 'Are you sure that's such a good idea? It might be good for you to start again at a different school. I thought you wanted to go to Larksmead? You could be with Penny and you said how much you miss her. Her mum wouldn't be able to stop her seeing you then, would she?'

Her expression darkened.

'Forget Penny,' she said. 'I don't need her now that we're friends.' This wasn't right. 'Anyway why would you want me to go to Larksmead? We wouldn't see each other then.'

'Kelsey' I said. 'I don't really know you. We're not exactly friends are we? I'm just thinking of what's best for you.'

'What are you talking about?' she said. 'Of course we're friends. We share something that other people don't. I know your secret.'

I wasn't sure of the best way to respond. I knew what she was talking about. I didn't like being forced to admit it though.

'I'm glad you understand.' I chose my words carefully.

'It isn't just that though, is it?' she said.

'What do you mean?'

'We both know what really went on in that bathroom. I've covered for you so far. I didn't have to, but that's what friends do. It's called loyalty. So I don't understand why you said we aren't friends.'

My heart picked up speed. 'I only meant that we don't know one another very well. I am grateful to you, it's just…'

'Just what' she hissed. The change in her tone of voice startled me.

'…just that…' *Just that I don't like you very much and you're scaring me* is what was running through my head. Should I ring for the nurse? I was quite a way from the wall where the bell was. I was being ridiculous. I tried to pull myself together. Kelsey spoke again.

'I could get you into loads of trouble if I let on what really went on in that bathroom. I don't have to protect you, you know.'

'I didn't ask you to.'

'No, but you don't seem very grateful. I thought you would be glad we were friends. Where are Cherry and Samia? They don't seem to visit you very much. It's because they don't get you like I do.'

I realised there was no point arguing with her. Before I could react she reached over and picked up my Blackberry from the table. 'I haven't got your number have I?' She tapped at the buttons and her own phone started ringing in her bag. 'There, that's sorted. I'll give you a missed call back and you've got mine too. Now we can be in touch all the time.'

This was not going at all the way it was supposed to. I didn't want Kelsey to have my mobile number, but in a matter of seconds she had got hold of it without me realising what was happening. My hands had started shaking and I found myself unable to speak.

Luckily at that moment the nurse came back in and announced that it was lunchtime. It must have been the first time I was relieved to see lunch arrive. Visitors were not allowed to stay during mealtimes.

'Visiting time is over' the nurse announced brightly. 'Leila has to eat now.'

Kelsey glared at the nurse, reluctantly picking up her bag. She stopped to stare at the tray which was piled high with cottage pie and vegetables. I was desperate for her to go. She took her time buttoning up her jacket but finally she was in the doorway.

'I'll be back very soon' she said, her eyes flashing angrily at me. 'Enjoy your lunch.'

As soon as she had gone I burst into tears. 'Oh for goodness sake' said the nurse. 'You know you have to eat it.'

'It's not the food' I blubbered.

The expression of annoyance on the nurse's face was the last straw. I stood up and shoved the tray of food onto the floor.   I pushed past the nurse and ran as fast as I could down the corridor. The place was deserted and I charged through the swing door to the staircase. I slowed down and composed myself as I got to the ground floor, I didn't want to draw attention to myself and be dragged back upstairs.

The lobby was fairly busy, mostly with people sitting around waiting, looking as if they had been there all morning. Several people stood around drinking coffee from Styrofoam cups. The aroma made me feel nauseous. I pushed through the main entrance to the hospital and turned left. A few patients were outside, smoking; some seated in wheelchairs or attached to drips. One young guy was standing alone. I recognised him from the psychiatric ward. He had always been friendly to me. A desperate craving for a cigarette drove me towards him. I hadn't had one for days.

'Can I have a cigarette please?' I asked him. He passed me a cigarette without commenting, clicked his lighter up towards me and lit it for me. I tried and failed to stop my hands from shaking. He pressed two more cigarettes into my hand.

'Chill' he said.

I inhaled deeply and slowly released the smoke and with it the beginnings of my anger.

'Thanks. See you inside' I muttered and quickly went off round the corner. I knew there were some benches there, away from the main road and the front entrance. I wasn't going to run away, I just wanted some space and to be able to appreciate the outdoors. I smoked the cigarettes and sat for a long time on the bench, trying to make sense of what had happened. Smoking calmed me down and I finally managed to stop shaking. I should never have doubted my gut instinct. Kelsey was weird and now she seemed to be threatening me. I understood the subtext of our conversation. It was blackmail. I was in trouble and I was terrified.

By now it was getting cold and I decided it was time to face the music. Reluctantly I made my way back into the hospital. As I entered the main lobby, a security guard I recognised from the ward came up to me. He had always been kind to me so I wasn't worried.

'Come on Leila' he said. 'We were just about to ring your parents.'

I gave him a sheepish look and let him escort me back up to the ward.

The psych ward must have been short staffed that day because I got off very lightly. After a bit of a rollicking from the Charge Nurse I was sent back to my room and put under supervision for the rest of the day, plus all visits were cancelled for at least the next week. That was a relief because it meant Kelsey would be kept away. I got my phone out to text Kate, she might be able to reassure me. I would tell Dora I had contacted her, that way I was still keeping my promise.

My relief didn't last long. No sooner had I got the phone in my hand than it started buzzing. I hoped it was a message from Samia or Jenna, but an unrecognised number flashed up on the screen. I opened the text and I read the words that came up before me:

'Blood Sisters together forever.'

I knew immediately who it was from. My blood ran cold and I started shaking uncontrollably. She had got me.

37

JENNA

PC Ellis was unable to visit Leila before the weekend as she had work she needed to attend to at the station for the next couple of days. I spent the afternoon at home in a much better frame of mind. I was still nervous about having betrayed Leila to PC Ellis but I trusted that she would know what to do. Mum was at work that afternoon so I decided to make the most of the peace and quiet and do some more research.

I plugged Mum's laptop in downstairs and Googled 'self-harming.' One of the first hits was an NHS site so I clicked on that and started reading. It said that people self-harmed as a way of dealing with difficult emotions that they kept bottled up inside them. Words like 'trapped' 'guilty' and 'ashamed' came up as expressing the way a sufferer may feel and I recognised all of them in Leila. I also found out about other manifestations of self-harm apart from cutting, which took me by surprise. Leila's eating disorder was obviously a form of self-abuse, but it was the list of other activities that made me stop and think. That awful moment when she had endangered herself by lying down in the street flashed through my head. I should have realised.

The site advised family members not to get angry. I sighed. It was so easy to give advice but not so easy to put into practice. I had to be super patient and not get upset If Leila did kick off when PC Ellis and I talked to her. That was easier said than done.

Fed up, I closed that page and went onto Facebook instead. After a quick look at some photos Mary had posted I typed in Kelsey Atwood. A list of Kelseys appeared. Rejecting the Kelsey who worked as a waitress in a Japanese restaurant and the young mother from Columbia, I soon spotted Kelsey's morose face staring back at me. Her dark lank hair hung down obscuring her face. I wondered if it was deliberate. I clicked on her list of friends to see if I recognised any of them. She had over three hundred friends but after a bit of digging it struck me that they were scattered all over the country, so I guessed they were random people she had met online. I recognised Lizzie, a girl from Leila's class, who I went out of my way to avoid as she could be a bit of a bully. I wondered why she had three different secondary schools listed. Kelsey listed her interests as Goth Rock, tattoos and 'the dark side.' Her main interaction was with the 'Goths Unite' page which was full of weird pictures and people. I clicked back onto my page where I started typing out a long message to Mary, who would be stuck in double French at the moment.

I had just finished typing when I heard a key at the door and the sound of Lily's voice. I hadn't realised how late it had got. I logged off the computer as Lily came flying into the room, followed by Mum.

'Hi darling' she said. 'How did you get on?'

I eased Lily onto my lap, enjoying the warmth of her

furry coat which she was still wearing.

I smiled. 'PC Ellis is great to talk to.' I said. 'I was so nervous when you took me in this morning.'

Mum nodded. 'I know you were. To be honest, going into a police station is not something I'm used to either. It makes you feel as if you've done something wrong just by being there. I knew you'd be ok with PC Ellis. I spoke to her quite a bit after the incident with Leila at school and at the hospital and I trusted her. Some parents don't like it but I find it reassuring that the school has a police officer on site. I wouldn't fancy that job myself though.'

'Well I'm glad we have PC Ellis at our school. She's going to take me to see Leila in the next few days so that we can talk.' 'And what about you? Did she help put your mind at rest?'

I frowned. Mum raised her hands 'Don't look like that, you don't have to tell me what you were talking about, I just want to know whether it helped.'

I nodded. 'It was good to get a few things off my chest and I think she will be able to sort things out.'

'That's good' said Mum.

'She talked about me being off school as well, but I think I'll be able to go back soon. I just need to speak to Leila first.'

'Ok' she said, 'as long as it isn't for too much longer. I'm going to go and get dinner ready now, do you want to help me or do you want to watch TV with Lily?'

'Watch TV' shouted Lily.

'It looks like I don't have a choice' I laughed. 'I'll come and lay the table in a bit – if Lily gives her permission.'

Mum went into the kitchen and Lily picked up the remote and started switching channels until she found a cartoon that she liked. I felt better than I had in ages. I felt guilty, as if

I was betraying Leila, but I was appreciating how much easier mealtimes now were without her around.

Next morning I was having my breakfast when Dad came in and broke the silence. The house was so quiet without Leila.

'Dora rang last night' he said. 'She's a bit worried about Leila.' My face dropped. 'No, she's still doing well' he said, 'but Dora thinks she has something on her mind as she seems very nervous. Since the day she went AWOL in fact. She's asked PC Ellis to go and see her, as it may be that the police investigation is still on and that is what is unsettling her. PC Ellis wants you to go too.'

When we arrived at the hospital later that afternoon, Leila was doing some homework on her bed. PC Ellis went ahead and I hovered in the doorway. Leila looked up and as soon as we caught sight of each other I rushed over and threw my arms around her, both crying and laughing at the same time.

'Hello Leila' PC Ellis said. 'I need to have a chat with you but I know you haven't seen Jenna for a while so I'll give you two a moment to catch up. I'm going to pop down to the hospital canteen. I could do with a cup of tea after the day I've had.'

She left the room and she headed off towards the lifts which would take her down to the ground floor. I sat on the bed with Leila, holding her hand. 'It's so good to see you' I said. 'You look a bit better – but tired. Is everything ok?'

She sighed. 'I feel a bit better physically' she said. 'But putting weight on is so hard.'

I was disappointed. 'Please try, Leila. I want you to get better. It's not the same at home without you. You haven't been listening to that Voice again have you?'

'Shhh' she said, embarrassed. 'That's a secret. Forget I ever mentioned it.'

'I think I know what it has been making you do.' I said.

'What do you mean?'

'I think you have been cutting yourself and that's why you took a blade into school.'

'You don't know what you're talking about.' She wouldn't look at me and the moment was disturbed by PC Ellis who came back into the room, holding a cup of tea in a bright orange polystyrene cup.

'Hospital tea' she said, placing the cup down on the bedside table, 'almost as bad as the stuff we get in the police canteen.'

I carried on the conversation as if she hadn't interrupted, before I lost my nerve. I looked directly at Leila. 'I wanted to do the right thing' I began, 'so this morning I went to see PC Ellis.' Leila looked horrified.

'I told her I thought you were hurting yourself.'

Leila stared at me. A look of bewilderment covered her face. I was beginning to wish I had never started this. PC Ellis took over.

'It's nothing to be ashamed of Leila' she said. 'Unfortunately in my career I have met many girls who cut themselves. It's sad but true. You need to tell us the truth. Are we right?' Leila put her head in her hands.

'I'm sorry' I said.

'Jenna did the right thing Leila,' said PC Ellis, 'but she's not the only detective in the room.' She flashed a reassuring look at me. 'I had worked out how the blade got into school too, but I wasn't sure which of you girls was responsible. I was waiting for one of you to come and tell me the truth. So how about we go through it all again now?'

'Leila, why do you have to keep doing these things to yourself? Not eating is bad enough, but this – it's horrible. Do you really cut your own skin?'

'Shut up' hissed Leila. She looked furious. 'How could you go behind my back like that?' 'You could have at least spoken to me first. You better not have said anything to her about the other thing.'

PC Ellis interrupted us. 'Don't forget you haven't been allowed visitors for the last few days, Leila. Jenna has had a difficult time and I think she was very brave coming to me. It wasn't easy for her at all. Try and think about how your sister is feeling. She only wants what's best for you.'

'It's not the sort of thing you can say in a text' I said quietly. I felt as if I was sinking.

PC Ellis continued. 'Will you tell me what happened that day at school Leila? The sooner you tell me the sooner we will all stop pestering you. I need to hear it in your own words.'

Leila shook her head. I couldn't believe it. Surely she would want the opportunity to come clean?

'Are you refusing to answer Leila?' PC Ellis sighed. 'You are making this unnecessarily difficult for yourself.'

'No comment' said Leila and lay down on the bed. She gazed up at the blank white ceiling. I wished my mind were as white and empty.

PC Ellis waited for a while. Leila closed her eyes. She looked pale and exhausted. After what seemed like ages PC Ellis stood up.

'Jenna and I are leaving Leila. You need to think carefully about what you are doing. I need to know what happened that day and you're not doing yourself any favours by keeping quiet. I'm aware you haven't confirmed or denied the self-harming, but I will be speaking to your Doctor about my concerns.'

I went over to kiss her on the cheek, but she turned angrily away from me. My stomach twisted into a knot. What had I done?

'You've done the right thing.' PC Ellis said as we made our way down the stairs towards the foyer. I didn't say anything. It didn't feel at all like that to me. I was utterly miserable. I hadn't felt this bad since that time in the park. Where were Stacey and her vodka now? Right now I wanted to go home, get under the duvet, and hope everything would go away. Leila was probably wishing the very same thing.

The Voice

Let the girl fool herself. She might eat but she can destroy herself in a better way. Just take hold of this knife... The self-destruct button has many different guises....

38

LEILA

It had been three days since Kelsey had visited me. The visit from PC Ellis and Jenna was the last straw. I was convinced I was going to prison. No way was I tough enough to survive that. Hospital was bad enough. I should have seized the opportunity when I escaped last week and run away leaving this mess behind me.

I had received several more texts from Kelsey on Sunday and I was starting to feel as if there was no escape. I didn't want to turn my phone off as it was the only contact I had with the outside world. Having gained some weight I was allowed to keep my phone on me for longer periods. I still hadn't heard from Kate. I decided to try again; hopefully she'd be having a lie in on a Sunday morning and pick up her phone.

I texted the message:

Kate are you there?

My heart leapt as an instant reply came:

Yes! How's things

Not good. I hesitated then added: *One of my school friends is scaring me. The girl I had the fight with*

Scaring you how?

Threatening to tell the police I attacked her. I didn't she's lying

I believe you. What's she like?

She's a Goth! Quiet Intense Scary. I think I upset her cos I said we weren't proper friends

Do you like her?

I hardly know her. No! I wish she would leave our school and leave me alone

Don't tell anyone about her

Do you think? I thought about telling my psychologist

No you mustn't!! Don't trust anyone in there they only want one thing to make you fat. Be strong and remember they're not your friends in there – we are. The PT girls ok?

Ok bye

I put the phone down, dejected and confused. Instead of making me feel better I now felt awful. Dora was right, unfortunately. I couldn't tell Kate that I was trying to put on weight. That horrible blackness was on me again. It hadn't been so bad for ages.

On Monday morning I had my weekly weigh in and chat with the doctor before I had my usual appointment with Dora. I was surprised when I was led into the room to see a tall, elegantly dressed woman sitting behind the desk. She stood up smiling and held out her hand. 'Leila. I'm Dr Levy. I'm so pleased to meet you.'

'Who are you?' I asked 'Where's Dr Dale?' The funny little man with the bushy eyebrows had been my doctor up until now. He was on a different planet to me and I hated him weighing me.

'I'm your permanent doctor. Dr Dale was covering for me while I was on sabbatical. Doing research, that means.' A vague memory of being told this when I was admitted came back to me, but that period was all a bit of a haze.

'I've read up your case notes and I'm very pleased with your progress, as is Dora. How are you finding it?'

'I want to get better now. Being in here has given me time to think and to realise how unhappy I have been. Eating is hard, it takes me ages, but I am getting there. It helps not knowing how much I weigh. Talking to Dora is good, too. Except…'

'Except what?' her eyes were kind.

'Some things are still hard to talk about. Like, feelings overwhelm me and I still hate myself and I miss being able to cleanse myself.'

'How would you cleanse yourself?'

'Vomiting. Getting all the bad things out. I miss that.' I

looked down at the floor, ashamed.

'I miss that feeling of being pure and light.'

'It's natural that you will miss it, but we can help you find healthier ways of dealing with your feelings. That's why you're here. Don't give up, Leila. You've come a long way and physically you are a lot stronger.'

'It's nice to have more energy,' I admitted. 'And not blacking out isn't bad either.'

She smiled. 'There you go.' She stood up. 'Let's weigh you and then I'll take your blood pressure.'

As I undressed behind the screen I tried not to look at my body. I would not let the disgust in. I closed my eyes as she weighed me despite the fact that I wasn't allowed to see the scales. Once I was seated in front of her again she talked to me as she took my blood pressure.

'You haven't put any weight on this week, which concerns me. I notice here in your notes that there was this instance last week when you ran away. What happened there?' She looked expectantly at me.

'I had to get out for a bit. Things got on top of me. Sometimes…I still get black moods and I get frightened.'

'Frightened of what?'

'Putting on weight, obviously.' That was the easy answer.

'Is there anything else worrying you?'

I shook my head. I couldn't tell her about Kelsey, or The Voice.

'Ok' she said. 'I'm going to speak to the nutritionist as we need to address this, and I'm going to prescribe you some medication to help with your mood. Wait there and I'll go and find a nurse to take you over to Dora's office.'

I liked her. She was easy to talk to and asked the right questions. I wondered why I hadn't put on weight. I hadn't cheated but I was afraid. Could terror burn calories?

Guilt was burning a hole in me after my session with Dora. I was keeping secrets from her for the first time. No way could anyone find out about the cutting. I took my diary out from under the bed and flicked through the pages. I was looking for answers but I knew what had changed – keeping secrets was my downfall. I had to tell Dora about Kelsey and the cutting. And Kate, and…

I started to write a list. This way, if I bottled it I would have the list to show her.

1. Kelsey
2. Contacting Kate
3. Cutting
4. The V…

I pushed down hard on the pen as I wrote. Anger filled each letter. As I pressed out a V onto the paper a shadow fell across my writing. I froze for a second, then pressed my hands over my ears trying to push out the buzzing that had started.

Mirror, Mirror on the wall

Leila's the fattest of them all…

The Voice's venom filled my head as its shadow filled the page. I didn't want to look but the edges of the shadow flick-ered insistently on the page. I held tightly onto the bedrail and cast my eyes up at the wall. This time it was enormous. I could clearly see the contours of the rolls of fat. It had no face this time but now I knew it was me.

The time has come Leila. Time to make a choice. You think you want me out of your life but think long and hard, Leila. Take a good look at your reflection. Is that really what you want?

'Go away' I screamed out loud, knocking the diary onto the floor, along with my wash bag, bottles and make up items clattering down onto the tiled floor. The Voice laughed, a harsh, hideous, howl of a laugh. I shook even harder. The diary sprawled open on the floor. That diary was my lifeline. I had to pick it up.

Don't you dare...

With a swoop I lunged to the floor, grabbing hold of the diary. Next to the diary was the craft knife, no longer hidden away. An enormous buzzing roared in my ear before the command came:

Pick up the knife!

I did as I was told. The knife shook in my hand, familiar, comforting.

Cut yourself deep and hard. Cut out all the pain, all the fat. Do it! Do it now!

Blood rushed to my head. Pain seared through the fresh cut on my leg tempting me. Defiantly I raised my head and looked directly at the shape for the first time. I gasped. It had a face now – my face, bloated and terrifying was staring back at me, the mouth twisted into a grimace. 'Leave me alone!' I shouted and without stopping to think I raised my arm high and threw myself towards the shape. With a howl I ripped through the shadow with the knife, from top to bottom and watched, stunned, as it shattered into little pieces and then evaporated.

The buzzing was gone. I listened hard. The silence was foreign. Could I trust it? I waited for The Voice. Nothing. My head was quiet, empty. My eyes found the knife in my hand. My hand was still, no longer trembling.

I looked back at the wall again, scanning it closely.

'Leila?' I whirled round. A nurse was at the door. She saw the knife in my hand and fear crossed her face, her hands flying to her mouth. 'Oh no…'

'It's ok.' I said, bending down and putting the knife on the floor, kicking it towards her with my foot, like they did on TV. Then I threw back my head and roared with laughter.

The nurse was looking at me, askance. 'Let me get the doctor' she said.

'No' I said. 'It's lunchtime and I'm hungry. After lunch, I'd like to speak to Dora. There's something I need to tell her.'

I looked back at the wall. It was white, empty, as if nothing had happened. Had I really got rid of The Voice?

39

JENNA

PC Ellis ended up taking me home. I was relieved but sad that Leila hadn't actually admitted to anything. On the way home I texted Charlie and said I'd come over and see him when I got in. He sent me back a smiley face. Getting that was a huge relief. I really wanted to talk to him to set things straight. I was going to tell him everything; I was fed up with all the secrecy.

We had been out for such a long time that Mum was already home from work. PC Ellis had a long chat with her and told her what had happened. She freaked out at first as I knew she would, which was why I was glad to have PC Ellis there to soften the blow. I had been terrified that Mum would be angry that I had hidden things from her or that I had betrayed Leila; I wasn't sure how she'd react. The three of us sat in the kitchen and my phone kept buzzing in my pocket; Charlie had seen me come home in the police car and was desperate to know what was going on. Lily had also been excited by the police car; in fact it was only possible to keep her quiet by PC Ellis promising her a look in the car after we had finished talking.

I felt absolutely exhausted. I hadn't realised how stressed I had been worrying that Leila could go to prison. Now that I knew everything was going to be ok I had deflated like a balloon. I didn't like leaving Leila with bad feeling between us. PC Ellis must have noticed.

'Look at you Jenna' she said, 'it's been a very eventful day hasn't it? It seems a long time ago that I came to pick you up this morning.' I nodded. She was right. I couldn't believe that we were in the same week still, let alone the same day.

'Is it ok if I go round and see Charlie, Mum?' I asked. 'He's dying to know where I've been.'

Mum looked surprised. 'I thought you two weren't speaking this morning?' She raised her eyebrows at PC Ellis. 'I can't keep up with these girls. I think you should go and see him, Jenna, put the poor boy out of his misery. I don't suppose you've told PC Ellis about your little escapade the other night, have you?'

'Oh Mum' I groaned. I was hoping somehow with all that she had just heard about Leila she would have forgotten how I had made a show of myself. PC Ellis looked questioningly at me. I quickly changed the subject.

'Mum' I said 'There is one thing. I think we should be more upfront with Lily. I know she's only little, but she does pick up on things and it isn't right.' I took a deep breath, it was important to get the words right. 'Leila's secrets started all the trouble and secrets have made this whole thing a lot worse than it needed to be, so I don't want to start keeping things from my little sister. It feels wrong. We should all try and talk more, I think it would help.' There, I had said it. I could feel myself getting hot in the face and was pleased when PC Ellis diverted the attention away from me.

'What do you think, Mrs Summers?' she asked Mum.

Mum looked at me fondly. 'I think she's right' she said and pulled me in for a hug. 'Now go and see Charlie, I know you're dying to. Tell him I'll treat you to a pizza later if you want. I think you both deserve it.'

PC Ellis stood up. 'Thanks for coming to see me today, Jenna. It's made it a lot easier for me to proceed. She was looking at me so kindly that before I knew what was happening I had thrown my arms around her. She laughed. 'Go and see Charlie now' she said, 'your mother and I need to talk.'

I rushed off next door, thinking to myself had I really just hugged a policewoman? What a strange day. There was nothing I could do about the row with Leila but Charlie I could do something about. I wanted to tell him all the secrets I'd uncovered; there were so many I didn't know where to start. I really hoped he'd forgive me and we could put the row behind us. From now on I was going to tell him everything.

Charlie was in the living room watching TV when I arrived. Helen let me in and I followed her into the room, suddenly reluctant. Maybe this wasn't such a good idea. I needn't have worried, Charlie jumped up and gave me a hug and we sat down on the sofa together. Helen was hovering in the doorway.

'Is everything ok Jenna?' she asked. 'How is Leila?'

'I think everything is going to be alright.' I said. 'I went to see Leila with the school police officer. I was scared that she was going to get into trouble. She still isn't saying much, but I think PC Ellis will be able to sort everything out.'

'That's a relief' said Helen. 'I'll take Olivia into the other room.' She winked at Charlie. 'Give you two a chance to catch up.'

As soon as she had gone I grabbed Charlie's hand. 'I'm so sorry' I said. 'Are you still mad at me? I couldn't tell you everything before because I was so scared that Leila had taken a blade into school and was going to get into terrible trouble. I thought if I told anybody and I was wrong she would find out and never speak to me again. And if I was right...' I paused for a moment. Charlie looked puzzled.

'This is between the two of us, right?' He nodded. 'My mum will probably talk to your mum anyway, but...' I broke off, gathering my courage together to say it out loud. 'I think Leila has been self-harming. You know, cutting herself?' He nodded. 'I thought if Leila was responsible for having a razor and she refused to say anything then Kelsey would be in terrible trouble and how could Leila put her through that? I had guessed about the self-harm and the blade, but I wanted Leila to tell me herself. In the end I spoke to PC Ellis because it was starting to affect me. Look at what happened with you. I'm so sorry, Charlie. I do trust you, more than anyone, but I was scared and confused.'

'So what did she say?'

'She didn't admit to anything. She went really quiet and refused to speak. She doesn't look well, Charlie, she seems so anxious. But I'm convinced I'm right and so is PC Ellis. It would explain everything, but I thought it would make it easier for her to confess. Do you think that maybe we have got it wrong?' I shook my head. I couldn't work it out.

'No, I think you're probably right' he said. 'Poor Leila.'

I looked into his lovely brown eyes. 'Can you forgive me for not trusting you?'

He didn't say anything at first, then reached over to put his arms around me and held me tight. I realised that I was crying. He stroked my hair.

'What a question.' he said. 'Of course I forgive you. I'm

sorry I was so moody. I shouldn't have put you through all that. It's just that I can't bear to see you upset and I wanted to make it better. I am shocked about Leila, but you did the right thing going to see the policewoman. I'm sure she will get to the bottom of what happened.'

'There is something else' I said. 'I did something really stupid that evening when you left me in the park. I bumped into two girls from school and they were drinking and...' I was so embarrassed I could hardly get the words out.

Charlie stared at me for a moment, then to my total amazement burst out laughing. 'I can't believe you're telling me this' he said. 'And I thought you were so sensible.' I kicked him playfully.

'Shut up' I said.

'I want to know all the details' he said, 'then I'll tell you about the time I decided to try out Dad's cider and fell asleep in the garden hugging the garden gnome. Don't look so surprised' he added, clocking my incredulous expression. 'We are teenagers after all – it's expected of us.' He stood up.

'Where are you going?' I asked.

'All this chat is making me thirsty. Do you want a drink – non-alcoholic of course? Juice?'

I nodded. Forget hospitals and police cars and drama. A quiet night in with Charlie was exactly what I needed right now.

40

LEILA

Something was buzzing in my head. I tried to bat it away, but it persisted. I opened my eyes. My phone was vibrating on the bedside table. It was flashing, warning me. I hesitated but the pull was too strong. I had to know. Kelsey. I opened the message.

We are Blood Sisters. Blood unites us. I know your scars. Next time I see you we will link our wrists and mix our blood. We will be united forever.

What the hell? I sat bolt upright. I was shaking all over. She should be locked up in here, not me. Why was she pursuing me?

Then I remembered. I smiled. I didn't have to be afraid any more. I hadn't been able to speak to Dora yet as she had been out yesterday afternoon, but nothing could shake my new resolve. Since yesterday I was different, my head light now it was free of The Voice.

A nurse came into the room with the breakfast trolley.

She put the tray down on my lap and sat down. She was going to be in for a surprise today. I picked up the toast and took a bite, chewing slowly. I allowed myself to enjoy the sweet taste of apricot jam that was filling my mouth. This was my medicine and I was going to learn to enjoy it again. Disbelief was written all over the nurse's face.

'It's ok' I said. 'I'm going to get better now.' I said. 'I don't have to fight any more.'

'Save it for Dora' she said. I didn't blame her for being sceptical, but I would prove her wrong. 'By the way, your appointment has been put back to this afternoon.'

Not again. 'Why?'

'PC Ellis is on her way to see you, with your sister.'

Moments later Jenna came shyly in. The nurse picked up the tray, her eyes scanning the empty plate. 'I'm impressed' she said. 'Well done.'

Jenna was hovering by the door.

'Come here' I said, holding my arms out to her.

'PC Ellis will be up later' she said, 'She's speaking to the doctor first.'

'Why aren't you at school?'

'I don't have to go back yet' she said.

I understood the words that she wasn't saying – until the police had resolved what happened between Kelsey and me, is what she meant. Well I could do something about that.

'Come and sit over here' I said. 'I'm sorry about yesterday.'

Jenna sat down facing me on the bed. She looked sad, which made me feel even worse.

'The Voice is back, isn't it?' she said quietly. 'You're letting it take you over again. It's stopping you from talking to Dora, and you would have talked to PC Ellis otherwise, answered her questions. We all need to know what happened, Leila. It's not fair. Why do you have to have so many secrets?'

I could hear the raw emotion in Jenna's voice.

'You're right I said, 'The Voice was back.' She looked questioningly at me. 'This is what it made me do.'

I rolled up my pyjama leg and shorts to reveal the angry mess that was my thigh.

Jenna put her hand over her mouth. 'Oh Leila' she whispered.

'Are you disgusted?' I asked.

'Not disgusted' she replied, 'I am upset. I guessed that's what you were doing when you were at home, why you suddenly started taking baths, but I only worked it out this week. To actually see it though...'

I pulled my skirt down, horribly ashamed. What kind of sister was I?

'I needed to see your reaction. You should be disgusted. I am disgusted, but...' I couldn't help smiling.

'What's wrong with you?' She looked incredulous.

'It's over' I said. 'The Voice has gone.' I told her what had happened yesterday.

'I realised that The Voice was making me cut myself too. There's no point eating again if I am still being self- destructive. I've made a decision to get better once and for all. I mean it Jenna. I'm going to tell Dora about the cutting this afternoon. There's just one more thing I have to sort out to make everything right.'

At that moment my phone buzzed on the table. It made me jump. The phone had turned into an instrument of torture. The text lit up on the screen. I read it quickly and gasped.

Jenna was watching me carefully. 'What is it?' she asked. She grabbed the phone and read the message aloud:

Why aren't you replying, bitch? You can't escape me, you're my Blood Sister

'It's from Kelsey' she said. Horrified, she stared at me. 'What's going on Leila?

I took a deep breath, and told her everything else. Exactly what had happened that day at school. All about Kelsey's visits to me, about her stay in a psychiatric unit, the cutting, everything. By the time I got to the bit about the texts I'd been receiving tears were running down my cheeks and the shaking had started again. Jenna brushed my tears away. She took my phone and scrolled through all the messages Kelsey had been sending me.

'She's trying to frame you! How could she put you through this? Isn't it enough that you are ill in hospital? She can't help you Leila. She's sick. You need to keep away from her.'

'I know' I said. 'To be honest it was a relief when they stopped me having visitors, that kept her away, but it won't last forever. Kate agrees.'

'Who's Kate?'

'A girl I met online.'

'Online? Do you know anything about her?'

I shook my head.

'I wouldn't trust anyone I met online. Leila, you're so vulnerable.'

'I know.'

'This is the best thing that could have happened Now that it's all out in the open Kelsey won't be able to hurt you. You

221

know what we need to do don't you?'

I nodded. 'Talk to PC Ellis.'

'I'm going to call her' said Jenna 'she's downstairs. I'm not leaving until I know you're safe and that girl is out of your life.'

She took her phone and went off into the corridor. I saw her speaking to the nurse at the station – probably persuading her to let her stay over lunchtime. I was impressed. My little sister was being so grown up. I couldn't let her down.

PC Ellis arrived within minutes. She sat down on the visitor's chair and put her hat on the bed, placing her valuables inside it. She took a notepad out of her bag and a brown manila folder. Jenna told her everything that I had told her this morning. It wasn't as difficult as I had expected. The fact that Jenna had seen my cuts and accepted them meant a lot to me.

When Jenna had finished talking PC Ellis took over.

'I'm so pleased you decided to tell me what really happened at school that day. We need some closure on it and now that can happen. As I said last time, I had worked out why the blade was there and now I can fill in all the blanks.' Her radio crackled and made Jenna and I jump. She pressed a button on it to silence the sound.

'As for Kelsey' she said, 'I am going to be speaking to her later today with her social worker. I have already spoken to both Kelsey and her mother and I have seen the reports from her last school. You know she has had psychiatric problems in the past, she told you that herself, didn't she?'

I nodded.

'What she didn't tell you was how Penny's parents removed Penny from the unit early, to keep her away from Kelsey.' I gasped. 'A lot of what Kelsey said is not true, or she has exaggerated the facts. She did meet Penny in the unit and at first they were friends. But very quickly Kelsey started trying to control Penny and wouldn't leave her alone. She started sending her abusive texts so Penny spoke to her mother about it, as she was getting frightened.' She held up the file, which was full of documents.

'This is all the information I have on Kelsey.' I frowned. 'Yes, there's a lot of it.' She flicked through it and as she did so a photo slid onto the floor and landed by my foot. I could see that it was Kelsey and another girl, sitting on a bed. I picked it up and did a double take. It was Kelsey with Kate, sitting on a hospital bed. In fact the head shot Kate had sent me was cropped from the same photo.

'That's Kate' I gasped. Jenna grabbed the photo and studied it.

'That is Penny' said PC Ellis, 'with Kelsey at the unit they were in together. Who is Kate?'

I felt as if the ground was disappearing from under me. I couldn't speak.

'Kate is someone Leila met online' said Jenna. 'She's been texting her in hospital. Leila I knew you should never go on those sites.'

'I think you'd better start from the beginning' said PC Ellis, taking out her pen and turning a page in her notebook.

Realisation dawned on me. Kelsey had been stalking me online too. Kate didn't exist. Kelsey had used Penny's photo – Penny was underweight and I had fallen for it. But why wouldn't I?

'It's called PerfectlyThin.' There was no point keeping any secrets now – I no longer knew what was true – nothing was as it seemed. I gave PC Ellis a brief outline of the website and the girls I had met and she jotted notes down in her notebook. When I had finished she put the notebook and file back into her bag.

'Kelsey has serious body image problems and has a history of fixating on very thin girls. It's part of her illness. She was receiving treatment but I understand she hasn't been keeping her appointments lately. Her mum has her own problems and so Kelsey can get away with it. Clearly she has been getting worse. This needs to be dealt with.'

'Are Kelsey and Penny still friends?' Jenna asked.

PC Ellis shook her head. 'Kelsey may well actually believe that it's Penny's mum keeping them apart as it's easier than accepting the truth but Penny doesn't want anything to do with her. I'll need to take your phone away as evidence. You shouldn't be allowed a phone in here anyway. Look what trouble it has caused. Plus I'll need your laptop. Is it at home?' Jenna nodded. 'I'm going to go back to school now, see if I can pick Kelsey up before she leaves. The sooner I can deal with this the better. I'm also going to speak to the nursing staff and security here; under no circumstances will Kelsey be allowed onto this ward.'

I found it hard to take all the information in. It must have registered on my face. 'You can relax now, Leila' she reassured me. 'There won't be any criminal punishment for having the blade in school and you won't be excluded. You haven't been well and I'm confident that was the reason you acted as you did. What happened was an unfortunate accident. On the positive side, it did bring to light the fact that both you and Kelsey needed help.'

'You will get help, won't you Leila?' Jenna said. 'I think

you should get your leg looked at.'

I nodded. It was a relief to stop fighting.

PC Ellis gathered up her hat and stood up. 'The best thing you can do is talk through what happened with your counsellor here, forget all about Kelsey and concentrate on getting yourself better. Sleep, eat and rest, that's my advice to you. Thanks for calling me, Jenna; I'm glad we've sorted this out. Do you want a lift home?'

I knew Jenna would be tempted by the offer of another ride in a police car but I hoped she would hang around for a bit.

'No thanks' she said, 'I'll stay with Leila.'

She nodded. 'Next time I see you, Jenna, we can have a chat about getting you back to school. Deal?'

'Deal' said Jenna. 'School doesn't seem quite so scary now. Besides, if Leila can face her demons and get better, then I will have to follow her example and face up to mine, won't I?'

PC Ellis smiled, her brown eyes twinkling. 'That definitely sounds like a deal,' she said, then turned and strode off down the corridor leaving the two of us alone.

'I can't believe Kelsey did that!' Jenna shook her head and looked me in the eyes. 'Can you really beat this thing Leila?' Was I strong enough? I conjured up the image of the shadow on the wall and how I had turned the knife away from myself, shattering The Voice instead, destroying its power. An image of Lily's innocent face sprang into my mind, her rose button mouth forming the words: 'Read to me Leila, you do the best voices.' She was right; I could choose my own voice, I was in control. From now on the only voice I would listen to was my own.

'Yes.' Our eyes locked together, held steady by the truth. I smiled. 'I already have.'

The Voice

The girl slept, at peace now. The shadow flickered on the wall. The Voice was undecided, was it time to relinquish its power completely?

Acknowledgements

I would like to thank the following people for their support and encouragement, which made this book possible.

Paul Cheetham, Ella Ruth Cowperthwaite, Molly Cowperthwaite, Keren David, Jan Donovan, Carroll Elliott, Rosanna Mclaughlin, Nariece Sanderson, Sabrina Sattaur, Emily Sharratt, Julie Sparks and Anne Williams.

ABOUT THE AUTHOR

Lesley Cheetham is a secondary school librarian at Elizabeth Garrett Anderson School in London. She studied French and Theatre studies at Warwick University. She lives with her husband in Kings Cross. 'Her Sister's Voice' is her first novel. She also writes custom poetry.

www.hersistersvoice.com